Insignificance

Insignificance

JAMES CLAMMER

GALLEY BEGGAR PRESS

First published in 2021
by Galley Beggar Press Limited
37 Dover Street, Norwich NR2 3LG

Text design and typesetting by Tetragon, London
Printed and bound by CPI Group (UK) Ltd, Croydon CR0 4YY

The author gratefully acknowledges David Higham
Associates for permission to reproduce an extract from
The Heart of the Matter by Graham Greene (1948).

Paperback: 978-1-913111-06-9
Limited edition: 978-1-913111-16-8

1

STILL when the man Joseph turned his vehicle from the tarmac of the road onto the brick-paved driveway at the far-end corner of Lysander Close there was early morning's coolness in the air. To one side of the sky hung muted grey cloud which was part of the night that had been and nothing to do with the blueness to come. The night itself had been unpleasant, too hot for easy sleeping, this coolness of the present moment was welcome while it lasted. He parked the vehicle and crossed to the front door with its scalloped double glazing, the patterns were meant to look like seashells, he knocked, heard nothing, knocked again, upon still hearing nothing knocked for a third time and now was rewarded by the sound of feet on the stairs within. The door opened and he caught a glimpse of baby-blue dressing gown. Down soon said the dressing gown, in reality Amanda Margaret Hollander. I wasn't expecting you yet, you are bad Joe Forbes coming this early, that was how she said it then she pounded upstairs. See you in a minute, go in there. From the kitchen where he had been instructed to wait the man

Joseph examined cursorily the tea, coffee and biscuits laid out that were Amanda Margaret's thoughtful contribution to the sustenance he would need throughout the day, which was also his first day back and not something he was very much looking forward to. A doomy feeling in fact filled various parts of his insides, part bafflement, part disappointment, worry, humiliation. Yet there was nothing to be done and at least he was prepared, for example the discreet cardboard packet in his worktrousers which Alison, his wife, had insisted he carry for safety's sake and which he in turn had sworn there would be no use for. Alison had won that argument, she possessing a combination of infinite patience and steelish resolve which might in some manifest as attritional bullying or passive aggression, no such confusion being possible in her case however since these qualities of resolve and patience were very much her own and nobody who knew her could possibly call her a bully, least of all Joseph who had been married to her for nearly two decades. Facts were facts, his wife's character could not be denied, she was a kind woman, a jewel, such people do exist, to the vicissitudes of life they respond by broadening their kindness, how they perform this miracle we would all dearly love to know.

The clock on the wall told Joseph the time, 7.50 a.m. Aside from the movements of a family of sparrows visible through the rear window it seemed that here in the kitchen all was stillness, the wooden table, the hanging mugs, the stillness was nice, a pleasant touch of cold, but knowing that today's task, this renewed interfacing with the world of money, would not be achieved by indulging in quietude he went to the kettle, already it was filled to the maximum line, he switched it to boil remembering at the same time a specific impression he wished to make upon Amanda Margaret, an impression which required hot water. From above there came flushings and sluicings, bathroom sounds, followed by more silence which could only mean the application of make-up. The doomy sensations inside his stomach eased a little, the man Joseph had anticipated them anyway, now around them like flames from a gas ring curled other emotion-thoughts. The idea of eyeliner and lipstick and whatever other transformative techniques were being pressed into use upstairs by Amanda Margaret was exciting him, they dropped a flutter into the spot where his lower ribs met, the diaphragm he believed it to be called. In short he was becoming aroused. It was a long time since he had last experienced sexual intercourse, what it was like he'd almost forgotten, and with the temperature as displayed by the digital thermometer housed inside the kitchen clock standing already at 22 degrees Celsius there was little in the immediate environment to dampen his desires. Today Joseph felt stronger, more like the man he had been and the man he believed he ought to be once more.

The make-up was not going on because of him of course, he knew that, it was going on because that was what women did at the basin every morning. It was something they needed to have in place before they left the house, Alison did it, every woman whose intimate morning routine he had ever known did it, it was a rule of life, imagine such rigmaroles being considered unnecessary, how unthinkable. Yet there was no getting around the suspicion, it was strong enough to be called that, that Amanda Margaret had a soft spot for him, for Joseph, and as such might be making a more especial effort to appear attractive with him particularly in mind. Again came the fluttering against the diaphragm, that convenient division between the upper organs of the body, the heart and brain, that specialise in nobility, vigour and improvement and those other lower arrangements whose purposes are steeped in vulgarisms, waste disposal or unapologetic lechery. Yes, most certainly the midriff was a sensitive area in the man Joseph's experience, most certainly it was a dispatcher of vital messages. Nothing would be doing for a few minutes though so he examined the biscuits left out for him and thought vaguely about the jet stream, the jet stream up in the atmosphere that was, he'd seen a programme on TV about it, the programme had made him worry, was the jet stream asleep, was it awake? He understood in some way that its torpor was responsible for the current heatwave, let us be careful however not to give the impression that Joseph was in any way an initiate into the science of meteorology. In the matter of biscuits things were different. Here he was both expert and connoisseur and this was a dispiriting selection, childish and sugary, what message was Amanda Margaret giving him by putting out these unmanly biscuits? Did she think extra sugar would help get him through the job? No, it had not been that kind of illness, people were always getting it wrong, he knew he should do more to set them straight but he did not like speaking about it, he was ashamed because of the weakness it implied, a strange sentiment when we consider the unprecedented esteem in which the sick and disabled are held by the voting-age population of these islands. Hello Joe said Amanda Margaret Hollander smiling. Sorry to run away like that, I wasn't decent when you arrived, you're keen aren't you? Something further was said as she came down and stood at the foot of the stairs looking into the kitchen but at that very moment the kettle came to the boil obliterating her words and a jet of water vapour gushed from the spout, plastering itself against the inside of the nearest window. Can I make you coffee? asked the man Joseph, recalling the impression he wished to make and pouring a cup for himself as he spoke – for during his illness, which had been mostly of the psychological variety, he had discovered in some roundabout way an advertisers' trick, videlicet that those holding before them in both hands a steaming mug of some reviving beverage or other present to others a more positive image, more likeable, more trustworthy, more substantial. Probably this small piece of manipulation worked better in wintertime, he reflected, still he wanted Amanda Margaret to think of him as substantial. Knowing such things was good in any case, it made you feel less naive, not that he counted himself as one amongst that tribe particularly. Thank you, I don't really have time said Amanda Margaret, but what I need to know Joe, what I need to know Joe darling, is whether this is OK, whether you're, you know... healthy enough for this. Pink-faced and discomforted suddenly she bobbed into the kitchen. I mean, I can easily get someone else to do it, what I don't want to do is cause a… well, cause any sort of a – relapse. Oh said the man Joseph quickly, hastily, blushingly, that's all over, nothing to worry about, there's no problem there now, I'm fighting fit. He lifted the hot mug of coffee close to his lips, he felt the bulge of the small cardboard packet in his side pocket, he tried to project upon her the certainty of his new-found health and virility. Humour was the way to deal with this, the sick not being known for their indulgence in quick-wittedness preferring instead to gather themselves for the occasional morbid stab which causes those around them to feel half-dead too. Do you think Alison would have let me out if I wasn't? At this Amanda Margaret smiled again, yes this was best, make a joke of it, draw the sting out of it, slightly cowardly perhaps, a longer talk would be better but she really did need to leave for work. About the kitchen she moved gathering the things she required for her day, keys, purse, hat, sunblock, don't forget sunblock, she seemed to be in four places at once, the abrupt jitteriness was gratifying for Joseph to see. I'll try to finish early Joe, come back early and see how you're getting on, would you mind if I did that? Of course not, that would be lovely, I can see you're in a hurry now, don't worry about me. Oh I forgot my phone! – upstairs she rushed again, downstairs she dashed again, pausing before him a moment to concentrate formally and glassy-eyed on the ritual of departing the house.

So there was humiliation in this but opportunity also. The gas-tips of arousal continued to fire and lodge in the softness of Joseph's diaphragm, they were not abating, to him she looked fine, Amanda Margaret Hollander, she looked more than fine, the make-up had been applied with skill, her eyes were dark and perfectly distanced, her cheekbones high and blushing, the lips teasingly well outlined, about her throat hung a simple gold necklace with a dangling bar that drew attention downwards, the gold was probably real gold, the blouse she wore strained open at the third button. More extraordinary were her trousers, not the tightness of them which was another thing altogether but the fabric from which they were made, a silvery-grey that changed colour depending on the viewing angle, the word iridescent is fashionable amongst those seeking vivid adjectives but on this occasion no other will do. Holding the mug of coffee in a still more reassuring and trustworthy position at the level of his chest nipples the man Joseph took a step towards her, his desire was dovetailing into lust, he wanted to examine in more detail these clothes Amanda Margaret wore and the fit they made with her body, far easier dwelling on that than upon the fresh humiliation of being asked if he was Up To The Job which he knew was what she had really wanted to say just then. As for this hurry of hers to leave – well that was all right, he had hoped for more of course, a little dallying, a little flirtation, a little standing-fractionally-closer-than-might-be-appropriate, it was something he'd been looking forward to, there was not much else, there was nothing else, the truth was he had had a bellyful of the bad times and wanted some good times, was that too much to ask. What if now he leant in, what could be more natural, a brush of the lips, Oh Joe, Oh Amanda, I've wanted this for so long, Me too, I thought this was never going to happen, Neither did I. The first unhitching of clothes, it could be fast or slow, who cared about that, then the sinking down and writhing together on the kitchen floor, for some reason it had to be there, how appalling, how reprehensibly disloyal to Alison his wife, how fortunate for all concerned that these things play out in the mind more often than not.

But Amanda Margaret, still standing there, the seconds going by, wasn't thinking any of this, being fixated in the first instance only on her watered-silk trousers. Getting into them had been easy enough, the button at the waistband had needed a small pinch, over five years ago she must have bought them now but she still had her figure, she was proud of it, she knew it was approved of by men. Yet the shine of the fabric was too much and today the sun would blaze. Sophisticated dove grey she had believed them to be at the moment of purchase, but when she got them home they just looked cheap and garish. The kitchen clock said 8.16, where had the minutes gone, we must pray Amanda Margaret gets to work on time since everyone knows the penalties awaiting those who lapse, stress in the first instance, starvation and destitution in the last, where would we be without these strict divisions of the clock. But why was Joe Forbes gawping like that and why was he holding his coffee mug in such a peculiar way? Hunched, the poor man was, looked about ready to freeze to death – in this heat! He wasn't bad-looking, nothing special, sweet in a way, too thin certainly, perhaps if he and Alison hadn't got together so early... but he'd been through hell. Wife and husband both, imagine it. And what they'd lost! That thing, that condition of Edward's, whoever had heard of it, nobody, nobody in the real world. The momentary irritation passed, it could not anyhow be called irritation, it was hazier than that, one of those dissatisfied moods that come and go like a breeze but it was definitely too late now to do anything about the trousers, she would have go to work in them. Remember everyone'll be wearing sunglasses today, maybe through tinted glass the fabric will regain some of its sophistication. I have to leave, Amanda Margaret said, good luck Joe, good luck Joe darling, why she said this for a second time was difficult to say, a surge of sympathy perhaps, I'll come home early, we'll have coffee together, I want to hear about Alison, it's so long since I've seen her, I want to hear about *you*, as she opened the door with the scalloped double glazing two sparrows flew from a bush in the front garden and Amanda Margaret shuddered, for in the Dictionary of Omens and Superstitions that Alison had given her back when they were teenagers it said that a sparrow flying into the house meant death and that sparrows in general were birds of ill fortune ever since chirpingly at the Crucifixion they'd encouraged the Roman soldiers to stick their spears deeper into the man Jesus. It's a shame Amanda Margaret Hollander passes only briefly through our story. We'd like to get to know her better, we'd like to dig beneath her upper layers and find the shiftings and hardnesses beneath, the nurtured memories of childhood farm holidays, goats suckling in sunlight, the metal-bar coldness of cattle pens, the dust and silence of unused barns, how has she ended up in this suburb of lookalike houses, what came along to deprive her of the pastoral life she had planned? Once seen with absolute certainty as a milkmaid smiling over the churn. Neither is there time to delve into that other fragment of her personality which is beginning to develop a belief in reincarnation. Maybe in the next life she'll be the farmer's wife, or the farmer, gazing across fields at her livestock. Oh, but if only Amanda Margaret had succeeded in throwing out that wretched Dictionary early on! Then she wouldn't have to be standing here when she's late for work shuddering about sparrows, birds no-one else gives a second thought to, or thinking that viewing the full moon through glass brings bad luck or that seeing a cat eat grass is a sign of impending rain or a hundred of the other insane notions that fill her head. What a way to go through life, the allowances you have to make and the circuitous routes you have to travel by, it's torturous. She tilted her head to one side, she gave Joseph a farewell smile, into the smile she put extra light and sparkle, he and Alison had been together for so long now they must be thoroughly bored with each other but what a terrible trivial thought *that* was given the circumstances, one event after another it had been for them (she knew more than he thought), the mannikin, the symbols on the mannikin, Edward's arrest, his first appearance in court, his last appearance in court. Dustily the sparrows dived across the road, slowly a car drove by, somewhere a siren sounded, the clouds at least were high and beautiful. See you later, call me any time, good luck, good luck. Away Amanda Margaret Hollander hastened.

All very innocent. But the situation held promise. She was going to leave work early, she wanted to talk with him, sit with him, hear his news, there wasn't any but something might still happen, for his sanity the man Joseph needed it to happen or told himself he did, more to the point he would have to make sure the job was done by then, tricky but not impossible, what time exactly would that be, he tried to work it out, gave up, too many variables. Anyway it meant he would have to go at it great guns. Then again she might allow the job to go into a second day, you could always come up with some reason and once you got talking about the technical stuff nobody could follow you. Silently Joseph prayed for the opportunity to come, silently he prayed it should not come. For if it really did there would be an awful decision to make though he knew already what that decision would be, after the illness and now this raw new contact with the world of money which brought its own attendant streamlets of panic it seemed to him more important than ever to bring about some circumstance upon which his virility could be hoisted aloft once more. Strong he felt, yes, strong, healthy, confident, a great change this, he drained the coffee into the sink, tea was more his thing, having rinsed the cup he took from the items laid out on the kitchen table a teabag, he scooped it up then with a spearing motion as if releasing a harpoon into the flank of a resting and precious sea creature launched the teabag into the cup, it landed just right, he let out a moan, two moans, Amanda oh Amanda, the sounds filled the kitchen, he laughed at himself but still it was important to calculate the finishing time, the sequencing of what he needed to do and when. Forget the fact that Alison had arranged this for him, forget the detail that Amanda

Margaret did not strictly need the work doing, forget he was being treated by both women as a charity case and that only a few moments ago Amanda Margaret had gone so far as to question, albeit tentatively, his ability to even do the job, hardly a vote of confidence. Yes, forget all that, an easy enough thing to do from inside the shell of his new-found health and optimism. A shaft of sunlight peeked in at one corner of the window, the clock was a tyrant, he stepped outside to fetch his toolbox.

2

ONCE the man Joseph had carried his gear upstairs and pushed it into a corner of the bathroom which was to be the day's worksite he was surprised to see in his hands a slight shake. He had not opened the toolbox for months and scrutinising its exterior now he felt the warming waves of sexual fantasy ebb. For hours hereon there would be no softness but only the sharp edges of the tools and of the job itself. Almost always it became a battle of one sort or another. He did not yet dare to touch the airing cupboard door and confront the cylinder within, instead he opened the hard plastic case of the toolbox, he would put the gloves on then spend a moment familiarising himself with the things inside, what was this fear, this reluctance, you would think he'd never handled these tools before or learned what each one did. Never mind, it was a knack, it was like riding a bike, once you got going you hardly needed to think, everything would come naturally and sequentially. But he'd promised Alison he would use the gloves. A long time he'd taken choosing them, the fit needed to be exact, it was exact, now before pulling them on he brought his hands close to his face, he examined his fingers and the tips in particular where the lacerations usually happened. Old woman's hands they were, the skin there and elsewhere was thinning, the doctor didn't know why, he'd referred Joseph to a dermatologist but the first appointment had been cancelled and he was waiting for a second. Anyway what mattered was that his fingers cut easily nowadays, the slightest nick would do it and here he was commencing work in the old trade of joining pipes and installing valves and stopping leaks.

Carefully he donned the gloves, he pulled them as close and as tight he could. Hands might need protection but still it was necessary to retain as much of the facility of touch as possible. With quick superstition he then sifted through the tools, the square-barrelled tap spanner, good Rothenberger, the 15 and 22 slices with their unchipped wheels, the slide for the benders, there the one size, where was the other, never could you find what you needed in the depths of this toolbox, hammer, screwdrivers, chisels, PTFE tape, then the sprinklings of elbows and straights, a chromium isolation valve, really they were made of brass and the chrome sprayed on afterwards, the Bahco spanner that never slipped – every hour in every city such tools are used. Plenty of gas left in the canister of the blowtorch though the nozzle itself was dented from having been dropped that one time. An unreliable igniter it had too, he now remembered, stupid to forget and not bring something to light it with. He'd have to go in search of matches when the time came to fire it up.

What was the first thing? Light, of course, let there be light. What the second? You got down on your knees. Always on your knees, that was the position. And now banish fear and let's get on with the damn job. Down Joseph fell, thanking God for the worktrousers' integral kneepads. He raised his arms and opened the door of the airing cupboard, with the LED torch that had been purchased on the same day as the gloves he confronted the hot water cylinder he was there to remove and replace, he sized it up like a gunslinger, a flash of levity and why not, the gloves being black helped the Wild West illusion – perplexedly taking in at the same time the pipes that sprouted everywhere. I need a moment to figure this out. After some concentration the workings became clear but what a tangle, no surprise combination boilers had taken over. Lying full length on his side he undertook a quest beyond the wooden support blocks upon which the cylinder was mounted in order to gain access to the drain-off cock and determine its operationality. A little valve with a square key head was what he was looking for, through well-established cobwebs his gloved hand sought, always they were in the most impossible places. This job of Amanda Margaret's was a good way back in he supposed, after such a long lay-off his customer base was effectively zero but if he could reconnect with the old men he'd be fine. They were interchangeable these old men, they dwelled in their thousands up and down the land so far as he could make out, they had the same views, they talked of the same things, how right they'd been about everything, the greatness of Great Britain. To get them to relax you spoke of *old money* which usually meant measurement in feet and inches though some-times touching upon actual currency. Along the thread of memory as he fumbled blindly came one particular old man, a customer in the early days, over and over he'd told Joseph about thieves breaking in, what did he have that was worth stealing, nothing, nothing except the wedding ring that had belonged to his dead and beloved wife and that was exactly what they'd taken, how could anyone be so heartless. Joseph had nodded though his head was under the old man's kitchen sink at the time, what could he say, he couldn't do anything about this stolen ring, he was merely trying to clear the pipe and get away at a decent time, a horrible job all told because the old man had been shovelling soil down there for years, then this old man whose dry bristly face came before Joseph now with terrible clarity, white hairs growing from his forehead, white hairs growing from his teeth it seemed, what an apparition, this old man had even suggested that Joseph let him off the cost of the sink-clearing work because he was so upset and his pension hardly stretched far enough as it was. Well, Joseph had a conscience all right but suddenly he knew the old man was lying, he'd been cunning from the start, later on it was confirmed by other plumbers he knew, he's been telling that one for years, he's had free work off everyone, don't fall for it, don't be fooled.

This search for the drain-off cock was a preliminary, in no way did it qualify as an overture to the task-as-a-whole, hardly even a tuning up, yet in it one might look for auspicious signs. It was a bearer of portents – not in the strictest sense critical, its state of utility or otherwise could determine whether the job was to be an easy or a difficult one. There, located. With his free hand Joseph churned the innards of the toolbox for the triple-headed cock key, a tool less interesting than it sounds. Of course he should have picked it out before getting his body into this snakish position from where it was difficult to manoeuvre. No, no luck, he'd have to withdraw and look for the key visually. While he was at it (pulling back, kneeling, standing) he might as well attend to the cold feed. High above sat its scarlet wheelhandle, imperial pipe, imperial valve, looking as if it hadn't been closed or opened in decades, additionally the whole assembly there at the back of the airing cupboard was encrusted with magnolia paint, this wasn't so good. He drenched the mechanism in WD40, careful don't get any on the scarlet handle itself, you've got to grip that thing and turn it. Give it a couple of minutes to soak in. Meanwhile after emptying half the contents of the toolbox Joseph found the triple-headed cock key then lowered himself once more onto his side, stretching at full extension around the yellow-foamed circumference of the cylinder which was, after all, an easier avenue of approach than going between the wooden support blocks. Nudging simultaneously beneath the obliquely angled stump of the cock itself a washed and empty ice-cream tub in case of sudden flood. He tried each of the key heads until he found a fit, he turned the key, the gloves were invaluable, the trick would be not to get them wet, probably he should have started using elementary protective equipment like this years ago, again he turned the key, this lying-down-and-reaching-around angle was considerably uncomfortable, uselessly the key turned, no bite, the drain-off cock was broken and dry. A hose job then, fuck, not at all what he wanted, whoever had installed this setup in the first place had forgotten or neglected to remove the rubber washer, as a consequence it had fused during the soldering process, a thoughtless piece of work, possibly deliberate, what a perverse and jealous bunch plumbers are.

What was the matter with it anyway – the cylinder? That it needed replacing? Usually in these cases there was a brown trickle, rusted telltale sign, or the motorised valve, micro-brain of the whole assembly, locked and unmoveable maybe. Here there was nothing like that, more proof should it be required that the two women had cooked this up between themselves, baby steps back into work, that's the idea, get yourself into circulation again, the word *resilience* had come up a lot recently. The message was clear, it could not be clearer, moping around at home is not doing you one bit of good any more Joe Forbes. But strange that the breakdown had come so many years afterwards, delayed reaction it must be, for the workings of the brain there was no accounting, one thing he'd learned for sure. Yes, he might as well admit it, it had been a full-scale nervous breakdown accompanied by minor physical symptoms, a complete loss of compass in fact though such things were not supposed to happen to men like him. Hauling his body out of the airing cupboard Joseph stood up, he tossed the cock key into the toolbox, it wouldn't be needed again, the cold feed had to be dealt with now anyway, unless isolation could be achieved from the tank in the roofspace that was fed in turn by the mains supply the cylinder would never be emptied, without being emptied it could not be removed. With determination he seized the scarlet wheelhandle of the imperial valve, invulnerable it looked up there, heraldic, judicatory, but the WD40 must have penetrated, he twisted the handle, he strained at it, nothing, he put his arm and shoulder muscles into it, still nothing, no movement. From the toolbox he took the grips and racked them to the most advantageous angle, again he strained, this time he really strained, now the blood was pumping, it was rising to his face, he swore, we can imagine what he said, not much was left out, from the paint-heavy shaft of the imperial valve came a grind, the tiniest movement, the grips slipped, they needed re-racking but that first movement was the most important, once that came so would the rest. The gloves however were doing nothing to improve his grip on the grips. He removed the left-hand one and placed it on a high shelf in the airing cupboard, again he strained at the valve, that was better, in old money it closed perhaps a sixteenth of an inch, another sixteenth, another sixteenth, backwards, forwards, freer it turned, his hand hurt, again he had to re-rack, such is the life of a labouring man, day after day his adversary is a thing, an inanimate object with its own peculiarities, then it's another, then it's another, the conflict commences without dialogue, progresses without dialogue, ends without dialogue, rarely does it intrude into the cloisters of literature. A moment later some snag of metal or sharp-edged flake of paint pricked the skin of Joseph's middle finger, fairy tale echo, he knew the blood would come, it did come.

The valve was closed – pray it might reopen later when he needed the feed back on. Plucking his hand from the airing cupboard the man Joseph glanced at the dimensions and nature of the wound, he held it close to the window-glass through which the sun was sending its lines of light. If he could get through the day without suffering a cut or nick... the thought had taken on great importance for him and now already this daub of shiny red on his middle fingertip. In truth the laceration was of the smaller kind, anyone would think Joseph a haemophiliac, he wasn't, still it stung, never mind, get things in perspective, no use crying over spilled milk, he stuck the finger inside his mouth. While the saliva set about its staunching chemical work he turned on with his right hand both bath taps and both basin taps then went downstairs where in any case he'd left his cup of tea and opened both taps in the kitchen sink. Six taps in the house gushed, technically it was only the hot ones that needed turning on like this but why take the chance, that imperial valve was hardly trustworthy. When the taps dried up, the hot feed that protruded at right angles from the apex nipple of the cylinder could be removed, traditionally and by experience this took a trice, the copper pipe being 15 rather than 22, with that the remaining volume of water could be siphoned off into the back garden and he could get to work on emptying the heating coil.

3

OUTSIDE someone was singing jollily, who, who cares, Joseph swilled a mouthful of tea to wash away the blood-tang while the wound exposed again to the warm summer air continued to leak somewhat. From the side pocket of his worktrousers, bless their toughness, bless their integral kneepads, he extracted with no little awkwardness the cardboard packet that Alison had insisted he bring, he opened the flap and shook the plasters onto the kitchen table, waterproof not fabric, how clever, what would he do without her. He peeled away the white overlapping film at the back of the most appropriately sized plaster, wrapped the dressing round the damaged finger and applied pressure until maximum adherence was achieved then pulled on the discarded glove which he'd brought downstairs with him, no, he wouldn't be taking that off again so thoughtlessly, how life insists on teaching us lessons just when we think we've learned them all. Only perhaps for the later fiddling with olives would he remove it, the delicate stuff where clumsiness would slow him down. No, there was nothing to reproach Alison for. Her view was settled, she'd consulted others in arriving at the settlement though never Joseph, with him she'd been silent on this subject which was the only real and true one, the subject of Edward. It was out of consideration one for the other that the never mentioning him had begun, it grew to a habit, it grew to a custom, then it was forbidden. There *was* a certain wisdom in keeping things on the surface (not that he believed it for a minute), the manner in which she'd cured her curiosity about Edward's current life might even be admirable, but he couldn't do the trick. And then she'd had help, hadn't she, her job to keep her distracted, her religion, the not-being-lapsed any more, that bitch Colleen, no it wasn't fair to call her a bitch, still she'd made trouble, a do-gooder that's what she was, what good ever came of a do-gooder. At least she was out of the picture now. Which only left the other one, the Special Friend who bolstered Alison's *resilience* and there wasn't much Joseph could do about him, after all how can you exclude from your household someone who's been dead for two thousand years. Even tonight, the evening of his first day back, some meeting or other was scheduled, some talk in which this friend was bound to figure, long in the planning apparently and therefore painful to miss.

The taps were sputtering, the pipes were empty. Joseph stepped out into the sunlight needing to go to the van in order to fetch the hose for this siphoning operation that he could well do without. The jolly singing he could do without too, it hadn't stopped, it continued, it crossed the grain of his mood. Frequently it's been observed how happiness in others spreads like quicksilver to those around them, in this instance it wasn't true, smile and the whole world does not necessarily smile along. A movement then caught his eye, always the human eye is drawn to movement, it can't help itself, it's involuntary, so much for free will, there, a neighbour inside a greenhouse at the end of the next-door garden, visible over the low communal wall. Between distortions of the glass encasements of the greenhouse and the rising angle of the sun a goatish outline was conjured momentarily from this neighbour, then it was gone, leaving Joseph to wonder if the man had legs ending in hoofs of the cloven variety, of course not, what an idea, this was a pensioner tending his tomatoes. Nevertheless the image had been vivid, it struck, it lingered, unpleasant, that was how the whole thing had started, for him at least, Alison coming to him late one night, at first she'd said nothing, she hadn't panicked, she was calm, she showed him the Bible that she took down every now and then, for her childhood indoctrination had never completely gone away. And there it was, tucked into Luke, the tarot card, Major Arcana, the Devil, image of Satan, stoker of damnatory fires, hairy-thighed, auroch-horned, a pentangle at his forehead, XV above the pentangle (this number fifteen being, now that Joseph came to think about it, the most common of all the sizes that copper pipe came supplied in) – a joke, he'd laughed out loud, ha ha, he took the card, turned it, pattern of lilies and roses on the back, he shrugged, looked at Alison, her expression, he stopped laughing, the Bible meant something to her, Luke meant something to her, most persuasive of the gospellers she'd told him since. The shock in her eyes, the lines of her

29

mouth set. Who could have done it, was it you? Not me said Joseph. Right here in Luke she said tapping the place, could Edward have done it? Why would he do a thing like that? I don't know. Neither do I, maybe it was one of his friends. What a thing to do, I found it twenty minutes ago and the more I think about it the worse it gets, it's deliberately hurtful. Joseph nodded, he had to agree, he couldn't disagree. XV had been a further clue, Edward at that time having fifteen days left of being fifteen, this Joseph hadn't worked out till much later, it was an irrelevant detail anyhow, they both knew on the instant that their son was responsible. And afterwards the Bible became more prominent in their house, it travelled from room to room, on show, Alison's idea of defiance.

From its hook in the back of the van Joseph took the coiled garden hose, he shouldered it and carried it up to the bathroom, also he equipped himself with a length of Speedfit pipe utilised in the past for the purpose of cylinder-siphoning, these tricks and eventualities were coming back to him but remember the time, the clock's ticking, the job getting complicated, if he thought any more of Amanda Margaret Hollander it was no longer the tight iridescent trousers which he dwelt upon or her tantalising promise to return home early from work. Before him on its wooden support blocks squatted the cylinder, obtuse, scrupulous, barely scarred, during the minutes that Joseph had been downstairs it had not magically drained itself, the cabling of motorised valve and immersion heater had not been disconnected, the encasing insulation foam had not chiselled itself away,

30

yet another task that he would have to undertake because the frame of the airing cupboard door was inconveniently narrow. Quickly Joseph turned his attention to the hot feed, that perpendicular pipe whose objective is to serve, to soothe, to provide with alacrity the warmest and clearest of waters to the bath-head, the basin, the sink in the kitchen below, to stand ready at every occasion that demands heated water, the defrosting of hands in winter, the washing of dishes, the lukewarm bathing of sunburned bodies, etc. Without mercy he took up his fifteen-millimetre slice, he clamped its jaws around the pipe, rotated the slice, its cutting wheel was sharp, the pipe looked almost as shiny as the day it had been installed, hot feeds always stay in good condition but already this one was severed. Abruptly warm water spurted from its new-made end and Joseph seized an ice-cream tub (he possessed several) in which to capture the modest flood. When it had stopped he took the Bahco spanner and next loosened the compression fitting at the apex of the cylinder, sometimes here there could be buckling but he met with no resistance, off came the compression fitting, he tossed the hot feed onto the bathroom floor and with the illuminating aid of the LED torch stared down into the depths of the cylinder. Very little was he able to see, it was like gazing into a pool at midnight, pointless to be staring anyway when the water needed draining off.

His scheme as already mentioned was to use the garden hose. Once the siphoning action had been successfully established it could be left alone and he could begin the burdensome job of tackling the heating system so that the upper and lower fittings of the great copper coil, the outlet and inlet in 22, might be disconnected. As regards our insistence upon these lengthy and somewhat technical descriptions, let's deal with it by saying that while objections are anticipated our narrator hesitates on the cusp of apology – the peculiarities of the life of the man Joseph granting, perhaps, special dispensations. Never had he seen one of these legendary coils, for they lived in permanent darkness deep inside each cylinder's stomach where he imagined them either as bronze and viperous or else white, engorged by limescale, or sometimes, less lyrically, as hormonally enhanced kettle elements. Entertainments like this helped to pass the time and when you got on the wavelength there was no end to them. Complex sequences he broke into discrete tasks, the longest journey starts with a single step, no mountain is climbed by staring at its summit, where would we be without planning and hierarchical thinking, still sleeping in trees, that's where. Joseph thought of these things, also he thought of the jet stream, he wanted to find out more about it, to him it seemed imperative that the jet stream be preserved, if it was malfunctioning somebody should do something to fix it. Sweat stood on his forehead, perspiration from his labours, a bead trickled down his back, had they done the right thing about the tarot card, should they have confronted Edward at once instead of pretending they'd never discovered it, the trouble was he'd always had this strangeness about him, the way he treated his two parents for example, so different, one face for father, one face for mother, you didn't want to push him because you never knew where things would end up, it was like he had iced-over patches where others had depths, or perhaps there was nothing iced-over, perhaps there was only surface, the more frightening possibility. The main question at the time he remembered had been whether the boy's preoccupation with magical numbers was serious or a put-on. Anyway – if there had been closure, proper closure there at the end, probably he, Joseph, would not have become so ill himself all these years later, seven was it, yes, he counted them, probably he could have avoided the breakdown. All hypotheticals. Edward was in prison, Colleen had joined the Sacred Heart lot, an insane thing to do in his opinion but he couldn't pretend he wasn't glad, Alison had sunk deeper into the arms of her Special Friend – and he meanwhile, *he* was struggling to change a hot water cylinder and daydreaming off and on about an unlikely sexual liaison with Amanda Margaret Hollander, most of which desire had vaporised in any case, what a flight of fancy that had been, keep your mind on your work, Joseph.

With the previously trimmed length of white Speedfit pipe pushed and secured inside one end of the hose he was ready to commence the siphoning operation. He opened the top rectangular pane of the bathroom window, this too frosted in pattern of seashells, another involuntary glimpse here of the neighbour, the man appearing normal this time, then threw out the unadapted end of the hose and passed out its coils while attempting at the same to expel or massage away any twists as these would only hinder the combined efforts of his two lungs. The ledge of the window was a good half-metre higher than the top

33

of the cylinder which meant the principles of siphoning would work against him to begin with but that couldn't be helped, this was the only option, I'll just have to use extra effort. When almost all of the hose was external to the house and he heard it make landfall, vinyl coils tapping some part of the rear garden path, he trapped with the sole of his foot the inside end with its Speedfit attachment, obviously he didn't want that following the rest out of the window, then looked in the toolbox for a bungee cord, there weren't any, use the G-clamp then, how stupid to do it this way round, really this was a job for two people not one. For one it was too much, first day back, and this heat wasn't helping either. When you were young you looked at all the middle-aged construction blokes and wondered why they didn't crack on a bit faster, you laughed at them or thought less of them, not that it stopped you soaking up every piece of advice they sent your way, then at forty-four years of age you understood, in truth this was a game for the young. Some portions of that strength and manliness that Joseph had felt in his optimistic moments down in the kitchen, portions which had not in any case been anchored at the most profound depths, seemed somehow to be drifting away, how was he to get them back, who could answer, nobody. He stripped off his left glove and checked the bandaged finger. A little red was seeping through. Resolutely he replaced the glove, I'm not halfway through this job yet, no, nor a quarter of the way either.

Into the hole at the top of the cylinder Joseph thrust the Speedfit pipe, pushing its stiff full length into waters that would never again be warmed by convection currents. Through the aperture of the unseen copper coil he pushed it, so that if at this moment of violation the cylinder had possessed a voice it might have recalled Webster, help, help, there's a plumber laying pipes in my guts. As the tip touched the bottom a soft tolling sound rose up and Joseph raised the pipe a fraction, if its end rested too square it wouldn't work for siphoning, there needed to be a gap but not too much, careful, careful. With a bungee cord that he'd after all spied in a corner of his toolbox he fixed the pipe-and-hose-arrangement in place, it took some bodily contortions but was quickly done, he gave a testing tug to be sure all was secure and headed down to the back garden. Time to begin sucking.

4

Hanging on the wall of the maternity ward is the clock, it's the first machine most of us see, dimly we stare at it, what is this thing, we've yet to learn the most basic geometric concepts, triangle, square, circle, let alone the numbers one to twelve, they mean nothing to us, many lessons are taught in the womb but not these. Later we learn to find reassurance in the homely tick, the comfy tock, we give thanks to those earlier horologists whose ingenuity gave shape to the monolith, who saw fit to cloak the monster so decently, from certain perspectives in no way to be sneered at we might go so far as to say that in our beloved clocks we see occasionally nothing less than anti-annihilation devices. Sometimes they give us more time than we expect. So, vaguely, did Joseph think as he glanced from the threshold of Amanda Margaret Hollander's back doorway to the timepiece in the kitchen, the morning was not as far advanced as he'd thought, it was still possible to do the job in one day, that day would be today, the gloom he'd experienced upstairs was overdone, in truth a touch hysterical. Outside he went, no hanging around. One can lose a lot of time in the contemplation of time. From the yellowing shrubs in the borders and the trees here and there sparrows scattered, this year there were more of them about, they moved in flocks, it was good to pick one out and watch it fly if your eyes were quick enough. But this was the such-and-such day of the heatwave (how lucky they were said the newspapers, hotter than Athens and no sign of a let-up, weather systems settled, barbecue prices rising) and he wondered where the sparrows or any bird for that matter went to drink. Well, he'd give them something, a cylinderful of water, that'd end their drought in fine style. With the bathroom now directly overhead he located the end of the garden hose and pulled it clear of the tangle that had landed on the path, he backed up, manipulating and straightening the hose as he went, a vexatious enough task since the vinyl from which the hose was fabricated was unwieldy and never stayed where you laid it, I ought to have brought the grips to use against the toughest and most recidivist of the twists. Then again the hose was softening along the entirety of its length thanks to the record-breaking temperatures and that was good at least.

The principles of siphoning were not in themselves worth thinking about. It was necessary only to know that a vacuum created within the hose would preserve the gains made by each individual suck of the lungs, that by this incremental method the water would be drawn along the bore of the hose until it reached a point where the natural forces of gravity would take over from the retaining vacuum, at which time the bulk of the cylinder's contents would gush unstoppably. But if once the vacuum was broken, it only needed a moment, that head of water brought thus far along the hose by suckage would fall back and he, the man Joseph, would have to start again. Hence the importance of preserving the vacuum. As for the technique of sucking, there were two distinct methods but neither would work, Joseph now realised, with hands inside gloves. Since the vacuum was to be sustained by the simple expedient of placing the soft pad of one's thumb smartly, wholly, and airtightly over the end of the hose, the fabric from which the gloves were manufactured could only compromise the overall effort, offering as they did nothing like the close and efficient surface tension that a bared thumb might. Because Joseph did not wish to spend the rest of the day with his lips around the hose-end in increasingly knackered and puffed out attitudes he took off one glove, again it was the left one, he was left-handed, this had always been the stronger, more confident and manipulable of the two he was lucky enough to possess, also the one whose middle finger had been pierced during the encounter with the heraldic cold valve. Half-wet and rucked-up the plaster had become, threads dangled from the edges, it was meant to be waterproof, it wasn't, sometimes consumer items disappoint us. Be sure to keep the finger away from the flux when the soldering begins, Joseph, get that stuff into a wound and you'll scream. These cuts in themselves were insignificant, it was the frequency with which they happened that worried him, try being a plumber when the tips of your fingers spout blood every other hour. And Alison would say something when she saw it, not forgetting the possibility of Amanda Margaret Hollander returning home from work in a certain mood, with certain expectations, it might still happen, such trysts are not unheard of though the ages have conclusively failed to identify bandaged and bloodstained fingertips as an aphrodisiac of worth. Such was the condition of Joseph's fingers that it was quite possible for them to be cut even by the kinked points of the hose or by its end-edge. He licked the bare thumb of his left hand, wetness would make the vacuum-seal more efficient, he raised the end of the hose to his lips, emptied fully the air from both lungs. Mr Forbes said a voice, you must be Mr Forbes, the van parked outside, a plumber, how fortuitous, can I grab you for a couple of minutes? What? said Joseph, lowering the end of the hose and looking about for the source of these unexpected words. The speaker was male, the neighbour from next door. I'm very busy said Joseph. I knew you would be, that's why I'm glad to catch you, it's very appropriate you know, Forbes, you plumbers are like kings of the world. Joseph did not feel like any king of the world standing there with the hose limp in his hand. What? he said again. Forbes, Forbes magazine, you know said the neighbour, it lists the rich people, how they made their money, what they do with their money, how they go about making more, Forbes magazine, you know, but then let's face it if you really were a Forbes man you wouldn't be here doing this would you, ha ha. Joseph was confused, only dimly had he heard of this magazine, it had nothing to do with him, on balance he considered the chances of his own life ever appearing within its presumably high-gloss pages as slim. Broken toilet you see, announced the neighbour, I flush it and nothing happens, there's nothing there, no resistance, the water doesn't empty into the bowl, I wondered if you could pop over when you have five minutes to have a look, a look-see I believe you call it. I'm very busy at the moment, Joseph said, clearly the man had not heard him the first time, rushed off my feet, fully booked (in the diary there was nothing, day after day of empty pages). It's just that I was hoping you might be able to squeeze me in, persisted the neighbour, when you pull the handle there's nothing there, no resistance, it needs to be fixed, grandkids coming you see. The siphon's gone, Joseph said, he did not mean the siphoning he was about to embark upon, he meant the siphon inside a WC cistern, there are two kinds. Is it close-couple, is it low-level, high-level, instantly Joseph regretted the question. Oh Lord, now you're asking, it's modern that's all I can tell you. Call me tonight, my number's on the side of the van. Yes, but it's just I was hoping we could get a date in the diary now... Joseph turned his back, he'd had enough of this interfering man, he himself would never have grandkids, if ever they arrived he in all likelihood would not hear about it, an extension of the family line had never been high on his list of priorities but now it struck him as another aspect of the Edward-sized hole. Pushing out the combined air of his two lungs he put the hose to his lips and gave a tremendous suck drawing up the hose as much water as he could, battle had commenced, he saw the neighbour still watching him, pensioner, spindle-nosed individual, how glad he was not to have fallen into the trap of jollity, the unfortunate truth was that in recent years Joseph had grown suspicious of other people's motives.

Yes, there were two kinds of sucking indeed, sucking with the mouth and sucking with the lungs. The first you did with the mouth, or cheeks rather, as when an ice lolly slides down the stick. That was the safe way of doing it but the vacuum created was small and once the mouth capacity had been used up it was over, nowhere else to go. No, mouth-sucking was not sufficient for the job but the other method, that of lung-sucking, frightened him although there had never been a problem with his lungs, his lungs were fine and healthy thank you very much. The essence of it was that once the resources of the mouth-suck had been used up, you moved onto the full lung-suck whereby you started high in the throat then pulled your breath in from the top of your lungs down to the very bottom. Lungs plus mouth held a much greater capacity than mouth alone. But the risk in drawing the water towards you in this manner was that it could arrive suddenly, unexpectedly, violently, in fact if it caught you at the full and final capacity of a combined-suck you might find your lungs flooded with water, then you'd be fighting, you'd be scrapping, you'd be drowning, the onrush, Achilles against Scamander would have nothing on it.

But he was only a single suck in so far. The hose-end successfully snatched away and sealed, the vacuum pre-served. Upon Joseph's head the rays of the sun fell, in all upward directions hung bluish-whitish sky, the early tiers of cloud had dispersed like smoke. He moistened his lips, moistened his thumb, exhaled, lifted the hose-end to his lips, a fraction of the vacuum was lost in putting it to his mouth, slowly he inhaled sensing the water in the cylinder lift some little way up the hose – then it fell back. No reason why, that he could see. Dispiriting. A flutter came into his hands, from somewhere a twang sounded in the centre of his head. Some people did this for a living, kneeling, sucking, they got paid good money for it and it didn't take them all day either. Again he snatched out the hose and thumb-sealed it, again he drew breath, again he sucked, again he sensed the slight displacement of travelling water, but strange to say that during these actions with their obvious similarities to an act of oral sex his mind scarcely alighted on Amanda Margaret Hollander and her tight iridescent trousers, instead he thought dispassionately of the word itself, odd, why was it called that, he'd never understood, the penis was never actually blown upon, it was sucked and licked and manipulated in other ways but blowing was not generally considered part of the repertoire. Perhaps it was because it was a job that made you blow, like an old-fashioned steam engine, made you shoot, spurt of white, yes that must be it, only in his forty-fourth summer had it come to him, how naive, baffled for years. By now Joseph was daring to hope that the water had been induced to at least clear the sill of the high frosted-glass window, for with each inhalation the cubic capacity of his lungs was diminishing slightly. Some rawness there too. Conquering this additional height was turning into the hardest thing of all, quite possibly by choosing to do things in this manner he'd made extra work for himself. The other way would have been to run the hose through the interior of the house so eliminating the need for egress via the bathroom window but probably it wasn't long enough to stretch down and around the stairs and all the other twists and turns and out into the garden. In design the house was ordinary, a suburban semi, in keeping with the plebeian paucity of our story. Now, as the man Joseph progressed the advance of the cylinder-water in stages, it had to be close, pray that it is, he saw abandoned beneath a shrub a corrugated seed tray. They'd had one like that, him and Alison, same design, same manner of abandonment too, seamlessly within him was caused a memory-amplification, in another garden the sky mizzled, in another garden he moved aside a seed tray, a disturbance of soil around the nearby shrub roots, it looked as if the neighbourhood cats had been using the patch to relieve themselves again. No, no turds, only a gash in the soil where fresh earth had been turned up then patted down. A small hump, strange, Joseph went to fetch his trowel. Something *was* buried there, he kneeled and worked the trowel around the gash and under the hump, clunk, it hit hardness, the container was laid at no great depth, almost as if it was meant to be found, not immediately but in due course, in due course. He lifted it out and brushed away the soil. A deep transparent takeaway box with something sliding about inside, a wrapped-and-tied bundle, the wrap was sacking, who used sacking any more? Peeling back the plastic lid he took it out, freed the thing from its bindings, it tumbled into his hand, for seconds he stared at it feeling he should know what it was but his brain not making the connection, then it came clear and around him the temperature took a dive or seemed to. Two arms, two legs, a body, a lumpy head, tied around its neck was a noose of brownish-blondeish hair, it was Alison's hair, of course he knew the hair colour of his own wife. An image of Alison, a mannikin of Alison. Crudely it had been baked from clay, the face was featureless except for a central protrusion that might be a nose, only on its body where patterns or shapes were inscribed had any great care been taken, symbols they were when he looked more closely, hieroglyphs or runes that he didn't understand, instantly he remembered the episode with the tarot card, how unpleasant that had been, Edward still remained preoccupied by certain numbers, then he looked up and saw Edward himself watching from across the damp mizzling garden. Eerie uncancellable moment. How long had he been standing there for? Again the temperature around Joseph dropped, for Edward was no longer a child, now he was taller than Joseph, presently he would be broader in the shoulders, for the father the time of possessing physical dominance over the child had long gone. What's this said Joseph, holding up the mannikin, knowing that by no trick of the reassuring tongue could he alchemise this into a joke, here there was nothing lighthearted, this was deadly serious, thank God Alison was out somewhere, shopping, Saturday afternoon. It's Alison said Edward. Your *mother*, Joseph told him. Edward shrugged, the shrug was not meaningless, his lips were set, two spots of red bloomed on his cheekbones, Alison, he said again determinedly, the effort to say the word seemed to cost him something, not my mother. What? Now Joseph was baffled as well as angry and upset, what could the boy be talking about? Alison isn't my real mother. Joseph scrutinised the boy's face, the man's face, in vain he sought for some sign this might all be a put-on but there was nothing, only the red spots getting redder and in his son's eyes a grim glaciality. Alison isn't my mother, she isn't my real mother said Edward. Who is she then? I don't know, but I know she isn't my real mother, not my true mother. Of course she's your mother, she's your mum, she always has been, who else could she be, I've never heard such nonsense. Edward said nothing, so brazen, not a trace of shame, only this hard defiance, defences fully up, but hardness like that doesn't come from nowhere, something building inside him, for how long. Did you mean for me to find this? Joseph asked. Again Edward shrugged, these shrugs, it could have been a yes, it could have been a no, Joseph stood up, Edward crossed the garden, closer they were but no friendlier, Joseph tugged at the hair tied in a noose around the mannikin's neck, Where did you get this from? Plughole in the bath. Joseph wanted to hit him, such an answer, but he restrained himself, he knew violence wouldn't help, besides he was feeling a little afraid now, for a second he saw Edward not as his son, beloved, but as if from a distance, all ties of familiarity severed, as others would see him, this boy, this man, still new in the world, what exactly was he capable of? Abruptly the distance snapped shut. I saw you come out of her myself, Joseph said, I was there when you were born, I saw your head come out of her – you know – out of there, middle of the

45

night it was, he put his hand on Edward's shoulder, no longer did he have to reach down to do this, look, has somebody been saying something, we can get a DNA test done if you like, that'll sort things out once and for all. Edward's shoulder felt big under his palm. They're not reliable, Edward replied, very frequently they make mistakes or come up with the wrong results, I've looked into it. If she's not your mother, who am I? demanded Joseph taking his hand away, it wasn't only the continued denial of Alison's true status as mother that angered him or even Edward's refusal to offer further information as to why he'd ended up thinking along these ridiculous lines, it was the phrase 'Very frequently', the unexpected eloquence, Edward hadn't picked that up at home, to what alien influences was he being exposed? You're my dad. Well I'm bloody glad to hear it!

Around them the mizzle worsened, it was that kind that looks to be nothing then you step out into it and you're soaked in seconds. Who'd speak next and what would they say? But something seemed to have set between them, they might stand there getting wet like this forever. Joseph meanwhile had to decide what to do with the mannikin in his hand, this doll with its carved symbols that had something to do with death, that had much to do with death, the only thing was destroy it before Alison returned from her Saturday afternoon shopping. Striding out to his workvan he took from the daily jumble the blowtorch and heat mat, he returned to the rear of the property, in the most inconspicuous and well-shielded corner of the back garden he placed the mannikin on

46

the heat mat, this was a private act that he didn't want
the neighbours witnessing, as he went to turn up the
blowtorch's regulator he dropped the thing, it bounced,
he jumped, bag of nerves, he picked it up to find a dent
in the nozzle though the gas still hissed at his command,
the igniter clicked but no flame-roar came, unusual in
a Rothenberger, again he tried, again no flame. Edward
watched his father's every move but did nothing to inter-
vene, he didn't speak, there was to his manner a detachment that had little to do with resignation, again Joseph
depressed the igniter, click click click, this time it caught,
he trimmed the flame, only with the steady hot blueness
burning did he realise how dark the sky had become,
only as he caught sight of Edward watching with eyes
larger than normal did it occur to him with horror that
he might be doing the exact thing that his son wished
for, terrible thought, appalling thought, but already the
cone of the flame was turned upon the figurine, Alison's
hair was smoking, she need never know about this, the
smell of the hair burning made him gag, breathless,
needing to breathe, suddenly in another garden under a
beating-down sun water exploded into the man Joseph's
mouth, he ripped the hose-end from his lips, the vacuum
no longer mattered, a little water had got into his lungs,
hands on knees, three hefty coughs and up it came leaving a slimy trail, what a way to earn a living. Sweating
from knee to scalp too. Dizzy too. Hyperventilating too.
When he threw the hose-end across the lawn belonging
to Amanda Margaret Hollander water burbled joyously
from it, through yellowing grass-blades the water mean-
dered, watch it a moment, take a moment to recover,

47

fuck, get my breath back, look the ground's too hard to be receptive to this unexpected soaking, it's water off a lawn's back, ha ha that's good. All the more for the sparrows gathering in the suburban trees round about, what powers of anticipation they had, what tubby confidence. Then he stopped thinking about sparrows or the unEnglish impermeability of the soil for blood was dripping from his hand, that wasn't soaking into the ground either, in the final stages of the cylinder-suck the soft pad of his left thumb had been sliced, how had that happened, he hadn't even felt it, well there it is, look, face the facts, it's considerably worse than the cut to the middle finger which is only a scratch when all's said and done. Hurrying inside he took and wadded a piece of kitchen roll and applied pressure to the cut, a wound must always be staunched before a dressing can be put in place, the wad turned crimson, he took another piece of kitchen roll and wadded it, that too turned crimson, only after the third wad did the bleeding slow. Christ but he felt dizzy though. Cuts to thumbs were the worst, they hurt out of all proportion to their size, their healing time was the longest of all the digits, longer still if one utilised them constantly as Joseph needed to, rare is the plumber who can do without the use of his thumbs. For the second time that morning he selected one of Alison's plasters, he peeled away the white backing film, he swathed the cut in sticky flesh-coloured material. Why did it keep happening? You did not expect your body to do this, you expected it to carry you through without damage or complaint until almost the end.

5

UPSTAIRS he went, refusing to glance at the clock, time did not feel so friendly now. A nearby window had given permission for a brilliant cube of sunlight to sit itself at the turn of the stairwell and as he passed through on his way to the gloomy bathroom Joseph experienced a pang of regret, for like all Englishmen he'd been taught to feel bad about moving out of the sun. It's criminal to be indoors on a day like this, make the most of it, soon it'll be winter, the things we're told in childhood. Undoubtedly we're made of very fine stuff in these islands to suffer such angst in connection with this one particular matter when others, our numerous adventures abroad for example, have left so little in the way of embarrassment. In the bathroom Joseph gazed down at the tools scattered across the floor then took up the LED torch and shone it into the apex hole where once the hot feed had been, the cylinder was draining nicely, amazing how much water they held, he could feel it move under his hand, a slight rocking back and forth, encouraging. But milestones other than the siphoning still lay ahead, the emptying of the heating circuit which would entail protracted fiddling with the radiator lying nearest to sea level, the disconnection of the copper coil's outlet and inlet, the removal of the cylinder itself, installation of the new, the battle royale with the motorised valve, the great refill, all these were yet to come. Certainly further delays could not be countenanced. Though probably he ought to have a tidy-up first, the tools were everywhere on the floor, nowhere to put his feet, always he'd been a messy worker. Joseph bent down, he gathered this tool, he gathered that tool, archetypal image of the doubled-over workman, he laid aside the big immersion spanner needed for the next immediate task, it is now our sad duty to inform the reader that this was the moment disaster chose definitively to strike. Already with the blood rushing to his head somewhat and the dizziness still loitering there now moved into one side of his field of vision a blur, a wriggling patch like lurid seaweed, in the breadth of his eyesight it was about the size of a pound coin but growing, for good measure his ears began to pound too. What a time for it to happen. He straightened up and waited a moment, what was the blur going to do, maybe he could work through this one, no, when he went to pick up the immersion spanner, large thing that it was, his hand missed, went right by it, he needed to loosen the nuts on the coil's outlet and inlet, no, what was he thinking, they were still live, black central heating water would gush, something else had to be done first, what, can't remember, as he looked around the bathroom the solidity of the walls dropped away, he tried chasing down all sharply defined things with his vision, couldn't, they kept moving, the lurid patch throbbed, to its right black tides of distortion began to lap, in its centre there now formed very distinctly a lightning bolt or electrical-looking discharge, it was tipped on its side, it zigzagged, it flashed, it was present whether he shut his eyes or opened them. Clumsily he got the toolbox shut, snapped the catch into place, big red clunky thing, he sat down on it, good height and sturdiness for that, frightening how fast it had come on, some people called it an aura, like the bleeding at the fingertips this never used to happen. With elbows on knees and head resting in his hands he dug the knuckles of his thumbs into the upper orbits of his eye-cavities, on the left thumb he felt greasiness of running blood, things were not going well, they were not going well at all.

Possibly the cylinder did have a voice, possibly it had several. And if previously the man Joseph had been unable to hear these voices borne on their sub- or supra-human frequencies now in the grip of the aura-malady which was not a migraine but had been dismissed as one they pricked into audible human sound, or seemed to. Through the twanging that had taken up mighty residence inside Joseph's head they came, they circled, they assailed, the constituent parts, the castrato pipe of the drain-off cock, I'm ruined, I'm ruined, I never stood a chance, the last breathy words of the hot feed sprawled on the bathroom floor, what a sheltered life it had led, every principle and mechanism of the cylinder designed with a view to serving it, never had it frozen, never had it corroded, the gratuitous and vicious attack of the cutting wheel had come as an awful shock, I'm dying, it choked, the poor people of this house, who will wash them, who will warm them, who will divert my expertly heated water? Not me, answered the bass resonance of the cylinder, I've been interfered with, somebody's only ripped my top off, somebody's only gone and sucked me dry, it's not like I'm getting my refills either – that bloody imperial valve's seized up, hasn't he, what a time for it! *We're* all right, declared the coil's inlet and outlet bullishly, let's keep things moving now, import, export, we've kept open passage to the farthest waterways for years, we won't stand for this backsliding, if order's lost we're all lost, without doubt this stout pair would have won the approval of the child of Bombay from whom, let honesty win the day, we first heard such mechanical voices. Inside Joseph's skull they droned and rattled, his hands shook, was the disturbance in his vision being accompanied for the first time by auditory hallucinations? Firmly he shut his eyes, he massaged his thumbs along the ridge of his brows, the lightning bolt flashed gold, why not admit that since his breakdown and the events preceding it he had come to live in a frightening world, bad things happened there, they were to be feared, here again was the proof. There was nothing to do but ride it out, so there he sat like Dürer's angel, surrounded by unused tools but deteriorated several stages beyond melancholia.

6

F ROM down below there came a knock. Some little time had passed, we shan't bother to find out exactly how much. There – again. Not a rap, not a bang, neither a timid tap, just a solid neutral knock that seemed to sound from very far away then nearer when Joseph focused on it. He stood up putting out a hand to break any fall or protect against a stagger, the redistribution of weight onto his legs was not as hazardous as feared, still he remained in a daze, this reaction of his was automatic, someone was at the door, he must answer it, that is what you do when you hear someone knocking. At the top of the stairs he gripped the bannister-rail, foretaste of old age, take it slowly, whoever it is can wait. Through the window by the stairwell neighbouring houses were visible, a slight heat haze rising from roof tiles but at least the TV aerials were straight, yes, he held a hand over one eye, tested it, over the other, tested that, the lightning bolt was almost gone, the fibrous tide swamping his vision had stopped coming in, yes the aerials were vertical, it was passing, what a relief. Somewhere between the third and fourth step as he descended a more familiar pain started between his ears, another positive, a regular headache, one always followed the other but with a headache he could live. Down the rest of the stairs he went, never mind the shuffle that might bring to mind an elderly or vulnerable person, nobody's going to see this, who doesn't have low points, in private you suffer them, in private you gather yourself, well may it be imagined however that the episode had scarcely bequeathed to Joseph any new treasures of energy or well-being. Once more came the solid neutral summons from the door. Only now did the question occur to Joseph, we must excuse him for his senses have been fuddled, his mind has taken a little time to turn from the general to the specific, Who might this be? Amanda Margaret Hollander of course. But the writhe on the kitchen floor, Oh Joe, Oh Amanda, that was long gone from his thoughts, there'd be no betrayal today, instead as he crossed the hallway to the door beyond which a figure was standing in sunlight, the scalloped double glazing making it impossible to know who, the excuses simmered up, he'd used a lot over the years, no he hadn't finished the job, unforeseen complications, a particular part needed, water pressure's too high, water pressure's too low, something's blocking it that I can't get to, whoever touched it last didn't do the best job if I'm honest, no I wouldn't call them a cowboy, not a cowboy exactly but, you just can't get these old fittings any more, they're banned, they're bad for the environment, that's what Brussels says, blaming everything on Brussels worked nine times out of ten. All these and more bubbled to the surface of Joseph's mind in order to help him explain to Amanda Margaret why he hadn't completed her job yet or even come close to it. Of course she was a friend but still it was good to have something in the bag just in case. Above all he wished to avoid the truth, he did not want to say, Everything's gone wrong from the start, the drain-off cock wasn't working, I have two cuts on my hands, one of them's actually quite bad, look there's the blood soaking through now, then I had this – this migraine – but it's not that, not really – forty minutes ago I could hardly see, I thought I was going to pass out, when earlier on you asked me if I was OK, healthy, Up To The Job, well I can't in all honesty say that I am, I'm not over it, not fully, the mental collapse's been made worse by this never-ending parade of new symptoms or that's how it seems anyway. No, none of this he wanted to say, out of pride, male pride, out of shock, out of a refusal to accept that he had not after all escaped the doomy pull of the breakdown.

But why would Amanda Margaret knock when this was her house and she had her own set of keys? Probably it was the neighbour instead, the pensioner with grandkids who'd tried to buttonhole him into fixing his broken toilet, fuck, that'd be it, the figure in the scalloped glass was unfemale in shape, why couldn't people take a hint. Joseph opened the door, despite setbacks he was ready with an answer, his wits were coming back, there on the sunbaked doorstep stood Edward. Hello Dad, a smile, Joseph tried to slam the door shut but already an obstructing foot was inside. For ten or fifteen seconds they then tussled, son pushing one way, father the other. The son could easily have won but unexpectedly he removed his foot, he allowed the door to be closed on him, perhaps these attempts to force an entrance were merely a joke, youthful high spirits, there might still be some of those remaining. Beneath the hot sun Edward continued to stand, the little arched portico that Amanda Margaret had had fitted over her front door, vaguely pastoral in style, offering nothing in the way of shade. So finally it's here, finally it's arrived, the unexpected caller, the inciting incident. Joseph's mind meanwhile had been plunged into a fresh whirl, What are you doing here? he said through the glass, realising that his son had no intention of departing. Can I come in? No you can't, tell me what you're doing here. It's hard to talk when there's a door in the way replied Edward, and here he had a point. Against his wishes the man Joseph found himself forced into reconsidering the role he'd adopted, the role of defender, barrer of doors, raiser of drawbridges, for if Edward showed no inclination to leave neither had he demonstrated any proof of aggression, leaving aside the foot in the door and resulting tussle which had really been playground stuff. The automatic, in fact thoughtless, act of slamming the door in his own son's face had purely been done on behalf of Alison, with her uppermost in his mind – but she wasn't here. If things could be handled delicately what reason was there for her to know about this? Was there not, when all was said and done, an Edward-sized hole inside him into which drifted with unwelcome, actually sickening, frequency, the good early times, the rides-on-shoulders, the ice creams, running from waves, the cradle cap, the lisp that had appeared and disappeared, the glowing reports of his first teachers? Could a more terrible thing be imagined than never again speaking to or seeing your first-born, your only-born, who even after everything that had happened was only really starting out on the path of life? This was the thought shoved down for so long. And this, here, now, might be the one chance available to him. There was even a case (Joseph's mind took a cunning turn), there was even a case for making and establishing contact now in order to more effectively protect Alison in the times to come.

He opened the door. Edward was wearing glasses! He must just have taken them from a pocket of the thin shabby coat he was wearing. They made me take an eye test, everything's sharper with these on. The glasses were big, the frames were thick, they imparted an owlish watchfulness to the young man's face. What do you think? Joseph said nothing. Truth be told he was still at the stage of shocked recognition, this isn't how a father-son reunion should proceed, everyone knows these occasions are filled with warmth and love, perhaps a little deference on the part of the younger man, dissolving as the years go by until the older man misplaces his marbles, at which time the son finds himself stepping naturally into the senior and more authoritative position. Such a time, however, is far off for Edward and Joseph, if it should happen at all. You don't look so good Edward said, your hand— Shit! Blood was dripping from the sliced pad of Joseph's left thumb onto Amanda Margaret's hallway floor, the plaster he'd applied to it earlier was practically hanging off, the aura-malady having given him more important things to think about. Anxious in case Edward should slip inside while his back was turned he ran for the kitchen roll, tore off a load, half he wrapped round the thumb, half he used to mop up the blood, a stain remained but it wasn't much, lucky that Amanda Margaret had laminate flooring here. Not just that said Edward, your whole appearance... I haven't been well, Joseph told him, today's my first day back on the tools, I'm fine now. He did not like this line of questioning, that was how he perceived it, Edward had always been sharp, nothing escaped him, it was a relief the boy seemed to infer from these words that nothing of a serious nature had befallen his father, a cold or bout of flu it must have been, something easily bounced back from, no need to enquire again. What are you doing here? Joseph said for a second time, and with the door now open he hoped for a credible answer. Can I come in? Not really. All right, I'll just stand here, it's nice being out in the sun. Peering out of the doorway Joseph looked up and down the road, this craning of the neck made his head pound anew, a tadpole tail of the visual disturbance still lingered at the shadow-edge of his right eye but he needed to see if there were any unusual cars close by, any marked cars, he felt the need to be assured, he was, the road was empty, the windscreens of the few cars parked on the kerb flashed in the sunlight but none struck him as suspicious. How absurd, did he think he was involved with spies, the secret service? Nevertheless such things had to be taken into account. The absence of a plastic lump under either of Edward's trouser ankles which he'd already looked for meant nothing, there are statutes against aiding and abetting in these islands, there are men to enforce the statutes, citizens who film anything and everything, upstanding evidence-gatherers, with a wince that he knew to be unreasonable he thought of the neighbour with the tomato plants and the broken toilet, pensioners were not like working people after all, they were a breed apart, too much time on their hands, nothing to do but watch from windows. And although justice, British justice no less, had ostensibly been done at Crown Court, i.e. the accused, Edward Forbes, had got what was coming to him, the process itself, less than clean, had landed Joseph in a place where his life-long belief in the integrity of the law no longer seemed so well founded. A mighty machine, the legal system was, it could crush a person with ease, in the courtroom he'd seen his life and Alison's life and their life with Edward mangled beyond recognition, deliberate misrepresentations, avoidable inaccuracies, the most innocent things held up for the scrutiny and judgement of all, and then at the end nobody had really believed that Edward had Capgras because even the expert witness, so young, a slip of a girl, doctor of psychiatry apparently, came across as sceptical, when questioned at length she'd told the court that taking the balanced view was an essential part of her profession. Well, it hadn't been like that on the day of the diagnosis, no, on that day in the hospital there'd been conviction, there'd been certainty, It's something called Capgras syndrome the consultants had told him, it's rare and we don't understand how it works but we believe it's what Edward has. No, there's no known treatment for it. I'm afraid it's unlikely to get better on its own. Sorry, we don't know what causes it. Our job was to make a diagnosis, an investigation, this was a tricky one but the whole team's on board. And Joseph could tell they were pleased, it was a feather in their cap, might happen only once in a career he'd heard someone say in a room next door afterwards.

How's Alison? said Edward, in the sunshine, on the doorstep. As if Joseph knew what to say to *that*. Don't go near it, Edward, he thought, unhappy, astonished, shocked again, you keep right away from *that*, maybe the banning order doesn't apply here at Amanda's but it's permanent at home which isn't exactly a million miles away, if you have a probation officer I'm sure he'd like to know you were heading in that direction. I don't know if you were but I could easily say it. But Edward gave no impression of being vulnerable to this kind of blackmail, there wasn't a jot of furtiveness about him, his clothes, the thin anorak-style coat, off-white shirt, slightly peeling trainers, might not be the smartest but he had over his shoulder a fashionable enough bag, a sort of satchel thing, and he looked healthy, Joseph had to admit that, he'd even put on weight. Who puts weight *on* in prison? Such changes, what a long time it had been. Alison's fine said Joseph. She's been promoted, area manager now, she's doing OK. Still reading the Bible? Edward asked. Joseph shrugged, noncommittal, on the subject of Alison he did not wish to speak, he did not wish to give out information. But he wanted to receive it, he very much wanted to receive it – when did you get out, what was it like, what's your status, the position now, the legal position I mean, you haven't absconded have you, you're not a fugitive, tell me, tell me. Discussion appeared impossible where they stood however, meaningful conversations on doorsteps being difficult at the best of times for there are always distractions, an inevitable sense of the makeshift, it's too easy for one or both parties to excuse themselves and disappear, not that Edward looked as if he were about to turn tail. Oh no, he'd come for something, he had a purpose, what was it, did he need money, did he need clothes, a new chance in life, those were possibilities, they were probabilities, the gaols of England are not after all known for burdening their leavers with undue resources. Where in the country had he come from anyway? Where have you come from? Joseph said. Kent, replied Edward, why can't I come in? To compound the problem of what he should do next (even communicating with Edward like this broke a potent if unspoken promise Joseph had made long ago to his wife) was the risk that Amanda Margaret Hollander might at any moment turn the corner, home early from work with expectations of conversation, Let's have a good catch-up Joe, it's been ages, not to mention an installed or nearly installed hot water cylinder in her bathroom. Amanda Margaret knew Edward, she had taken sides against Edward, painful memory, being superstitious in nature she was bound to see his reappearance as a bad omen, to give her her due she'd probably be right, in any case she would be involved immediately. And then she did have that narrow but undeniable streak of mean-spiritedness about her, something in life thwarted, it didn't come out often but still it was easy for Joseph to imagine the phone conversation that would very quickly take place between the two women. Alison would be destroyed afresh and perhaps this time not even the Special Friend, dead these two thousand years, would bring her back.

He had not expected this to be a day of decision. Not a decision like this. Inside him there existed a golden balance, a golden and perfected set of scales, maybe everyone has them, if only they could be brought out and applied universally a fairer and more equitable world would undoubtedly come into existence. Onto each fault-less pan Joseph heaped weights and factors, Yes this side, No that side, the complications of Amanda Margaret, of Alison who needed protection, of the Law which could never be escaped, these fell on one side, on the other side fell Edward and the Edward-sized hole and the Capgras diagnosis, they were heavy, they were very heavy. He dug into the pockets of his worktrousers, he felt a squashed brass olive that needed to be thrown away, a scrap of PTFE tape, a grain of soil, he pulled out his keys, Sit in the van, if you see Amanda put your head down, I need ten minutes to finish up.

7

He gathered the plasters from the kitchen table and went upstairs. The cylinder job was over. He'd make everything safe with Speedfit caps, get the water on again, then write a note to Amanda Margaret. He had no idea what to say in the note, the only thing that came to mind was funny turn, I had to leave early because I had a funny turn, it might be true but what an old-womanly way of putting it, nobody had funny turns any more, they had specific and accurately described medical conditions. But this cylinder... he shouldn't have taken it on on his first day back. Not easy to believe that during the blaze and confusion of the aura-malady the whole apparatus had seemed to separate like creatures in a rock pool and speak in jumbled voices. What was this, the sixth time, the seventh time that the migraine-which-wasn't-a-migraine had come? Usually they lasted between two and three hours, this one had been shorter, that was lucky, maybe Joseph's entitled to hope they'll go away altogether one day. He applied the Speedfit caps, how well named, the cold feed could be left hanging, the place where he'd cut into the hot water feed was fine to leave too. The outlet and inlet in 22, the motorised valve sitting in its nexus of pipes, all waited for another time. If Amanda Margaret wanted to wash tonight the electric shower dangling over the bath would have to suffice. He would write a good note, yes, make her feel sympathy for him but the phrase Not Up To The Job, the five terrible words, those he'd keep to his secret self. Try not to dwell on it, it was going to be another hot night anyway, who wanted steamy baths. Just so long as she did not appear in the next few minutes. He hurried, he collected the tools and slung them in the toolbox, tomorrow he'd come back and finish the job, if any fuss was made he knew he could rely on Alison to smooth things over, he turned on the mains and checked for leaks, there were none, then a quick sweep-up with a dustpan and brush found under Amanda Margaret's kitchen sink and he closed the door of the airing cupboard, his head hurting again from all the bending and running about. On a pad of paper in the hall he wrote a heart-rending note, suddenly in the note he was articulate, where had that come from. When he was sat behind the wheel of the van he took from Edward the keys, they were hot from being held tightly, it did not occur to Joseph that his son had come from a world where possession of keys are of the greatest importance, he started the engine, he backed the van out of Amanda Margaret's driveway, no thought of where to next, somewhere, somewhere for sure. Let's follow and find out.

8

THE need to mention the weather, to make a complaint in fact, has been pressing for some time so we might as well deal with it now, this moment is as good as any other. Shorter days past the autumn equinox would surely have permitted more atmosphere to enter into our story of Joseph and his family. Instead, alas, we have a blazing summer's early afternoon, not a single cloud, and nothing even to compensate in the way of unfettered sexuality. As usual the English weather has shown itself to be unreliable, hear the news. Neither were the heat and light doing much for Joseph's headache. How did you know where to find me he said, for only now did it strike him that Edward's knocking on Amanda Margaret's door and no other was a feat in itself. His whereabouts could not have been passed on by Alison, so how had Edward known? I went over to Tate's and asked Edward said, Do you know Joe Forbes I said, do you know where he's working today? I knew you would've been in there first thing for your bits, Is he still driving a Berlingo? I didn't recognise the guy behind the counter. Somewhere round

Lancaster Road I think, this guy told me, I walked around looking for your van then I remembered Amanda's place, bingo. Clever, Joseph thought but said nothing. Taking his eyes off the road he snatched a glance across at Edward, still it was difficult to believe he was really here, how old must he be now, let's see, twenty-four, no twenty-five, twenty-five it had to be, his height, his weight, truly he was no longer their baby, and those glasses! Through the nearside lens he saw a speck of dust stuck between eyelashes, right from the start Edward had long lashes, girl-like, mascara-like. Only many years later had Joseph been forced to acknowledge the grave preoccupation of the eyes fringed by those lashes. For example Edward had never taken part in banter, it held no interest for him, this his father saw as a great disability, where were you in life, where could you begin, where could you go, without the small talk, the icebreaker, the little joke that puts someone at their ease, not doing it makes you different, it makes you difficult, it's refusing to play the game, within a minute or so of the knock on the door Joseph had seen that this aspect of Edward remained unchanged by his prison experience. Which was not at all the same as saying his son lacked chameleon-like qualities, those he had in plentiful supply when he wanted them.

Could the cab of the van serve as a cockpit of reconciliation? Hope, they say, springs eternal, one of our most treasured phrases, though possibly this isn't the place to dwell on the somewhat provincial understanding of time and space that it implies. The engine at least made a companionable noise, the seats were soft, the road quiet, the privacy complete, father and son joined together in the common endeavour of travelling side by side with no adversarial eye contact having to be made. Why didn't you come to see me? asked Edward. What a question. Straight to the point. They kept moving you about, Joseph said, I didn't know where you were half the time, Scotland for a while wasn't it? It sounded unconvincing, he knew it sounded unconvincing, in the many imagined conversations he'd had with Edward it had always been him, the father, questioning the son, never the other way round, now this, so direct, it put Joseph on the back foot, it disabled him. The *correct* answer, the answer that Alison and anyone else in living society would give was, After what you did! What planet are you living on? But Joseph's full and truthful answer, should he ever have the courage to say it out loud, was different, yes, after what you did was one part of it but another part was, I had to forget you, I had to bury you away, staying close to those things that damage you isn't really the best way of getting better, is it, because in case you were wondering, maybe you weren't but just in case you were, both of us had to heal after what you put us through, in fact some of us still aren't back to full health. The reason I didn't visit wasn't through a lack of compassion towards you personally, on that score you might be surprised, it was because it would probably have destroyed me, there's the reality for you. I wasn't obliged to, so I didn't, I had to concentrate on shutting down, I had to take care of Alison, I had to take care of myself.

But instead he had given this cowardly and confused answer about not knowing which part of the prison system Edward had been in. You could easily've found out, Edward replied, a couple of phone calls would have done it, I wouldn't have minded a letter or two either. Yet he seemed to bear Joseph no ill will, the question had been bluntly put for sure but with curiosity rather than reproach, that detachment again, that self-sufficient streak, how unlike me he is, blood isn't always thicker than water, Joseph reflected sadly, family does not always come first. What a joke that was when it came to Alison. Does Edward still see it – see her – in the same way? I must find out. But first things first, the ground needed to be cleared, the legal status of his son established. When did you get out? he asked, half expecting a police car to come thundering up behind them that very moment. Six months ago. Six! I've been in a hostel place with a tag, having to report all the time, seven o'clock curfew, you know. (No, Joseph didn't know.) Well, now the tag's off, no more curfew, I can go wherever I like – I saw you looking at my ankles when you opened the door back there, by the way. This casual matter-of-factness Joseph found depressing, his son had gone into Her Majesty's penal system a boy and come out a man, what father would choose such an education, goodness knows what he'd seen and what he'd been through. If Joseph's only ideas of prison were from TV he knew as well that these were unlikely to be accurate. The most disconcerting thing of all however was the way Edward showed no outward sign of anger at the years he'd never get back, the years lost forever, those specific years more to the point which large percentages of the population frequently declare in hindsight to be

68

the very acme of life. You should never have been sent anywhere like that in the first place, Joseph said, you should have gone, I don't know... somewhere else. The loony bin, you mean? No, I didn't mean that, but they should've gone easy on you, they made you out to be something you weren't, it's not your fault is it, what with the Capgras and everything. To this Edward made no reply, perhaps he shrugged slightly, Joseph had spoken the disease-word loud and daringly in order to witness the reaction but just then a car coming round the bend distracted him. I kept my head down and stayed away from the drugs, but what they couldn't understand in any of the places I was at was why I didn't want to be called Eddie, or Ted or Teddy, they tried to get it going but I told them, It's Edward, Edward, I insisted on that, after a few months they got bored of it, irritated but bored.

The town where Joseph lived and Edward had grown up was not large, previously we referred to it as a suburb, a better name might be satellite town, that captures its marginal essence. By now they had reached the outer limit, the buildings on either side of the road were gone, verdantly a hedgerow pressed in, its wilder spikes and brambles needed tackling, some tree branches too, since a couple whipped the top of the van as it passed by. It may also have been that the man Joseph was speeding, for if a well-known aspect of anxiety is that it causes us to do certain things without realising it, lost as we are in spells of preoccupation, the pressing monoto- nously of an accelerator pedal might serve as a good illustrating example. Neither was this a geographically exciting part of the world, here there were no cliffs or beaches, the hills were small, in truth they didn't do enough to even qualify as hills, the houses were of those boxlike kind that some see fit to stand in high-minded judgement upon, there were no old churches and if there had been no-one would be interested in them, the local library had shut down, the swimming baths were long gone, no knight had ever built a castle here, there were no colleges of learning, great or ungreat, the nearest cinema was seventeen miles away and those seedbeds of coffeeshop and cafe-bar everywhere rampant here went unfertilised. Up ahead came a sign for Barrows Wood which passed locally for a beauty spot. Joseph hadn't expected it so soon but instinctively he pushed the indicator lever down and turned in, ages since he'd been here, the gravel car park was almost empty, good, just what he wanted, plus it would be a relief to be under the trees, in cool, in shade, his headache might improve away from the light and stifling air of the cab. Edward seemed happy with the choice or at least made no complaint. And in Joseph's mind another idea was solid, who knows from what matrices of lived or viewed experience it had come, that meaningful conversations ought to take place in picturesque surroundings, ideally some vantage point where one could see for unobstructed miles, well there was nothing like that here so this would have to do. Edward gets you more respect anyway, Edward said as he stepped out of the van, now parked, now locked, now left behind, obviously this thing about being called Edward rather than Ed or Eddie was playing on his mind. Together they set out on one of the tracks that led away from the car park, the trees made a tunnel of dark green, spots of sunshine played on the heat-cracked mud of the path, forest flowers were in bloom, yellow, pink, blue, ivy twined in every place you looked, the general picture is a familiar one, we shan't go on, the last thing anyone needs is more nature writers. Meanwhile the countless conversations that had played out in mind-pictures and thought-words during the years of Edward's incarceration fell on Joseph in an immense babble impossible to separate, except to know that always they led to the asking of two questions, Who do you think she is now, What are your intentions towards her? But how to get to these questions, how to ask them in such a way that Edward would have no choice but to give an honest answer, would *want* to give an honest answer he couldn't yet see, the boy intimidated him a little, his health, his experience, maybe it would just happen, let's listen in to what Edward's saying, he wants to talk some more about prison and why not, seven years is a long time in anyone's life.

Raise your arms, stand there, do what I say said Edward under the trees, that's the first thing that happens. By then you're naked of course. If the screw's a decent one he'll search your top half first and let you put your shirt back on, if he's a bastard he'll make you strip right down, looking for contraband he says but really he's making sure you know who's boss. Pull your foreskin back he says, so you pull it back and he has a look,

71

then he goes and gets his mate and they both have a good laugh, Never seen one that small, we should take a photo and put it online, tiny penises we have seen, there've been lots but this one needs a magnifying glass. A microscope you mean, weird shape too, good luck son, you'll be needing it with that. Are you sure you want to hear this, Dad, it's just what happened but I don't want to shock you. Joseph nodded, Carry on, his heart was breaking to hear his only child talk like this, at the same time he knew Edward was getting a kick out of recounting it, this story called my first day in prison, a tale to scare the old folks. Refusing to hear it through would be seen as weakness, that was what this malicious little test was about, did he have the stomach for it. Then open your legs says this screw, squat down, here's a surprise for you, they have this special mirror they use to look up your anus, again he takes a good look, Amazing what you can hide and where, he says. He looks clean to me, says the other. Filthy disgusting I'd say but it's no business of mine says the first one, this is in reception remember, before they've even taken you to your cell. The path became uneven, Edward trod carefully, his peeling trainers were not in need of any more wear. The funny thing is, it really is amazing what you can get up there – up the anus, I mean. All sorts of stuff gets in that way. I even knew this bloke once who put an energy drink up there. He only did it because he was bored, he walked around for a bit like that, not too long, well you can imagine can't you, then he took it out, or it came out, and he offered to share it with this new member of staff. Screw drank nearly the whole thing, thought he was making friends with the cons, you know, building relationships, starting off on the good foot, ha!

But Edward wasn't laughing or even smiling at his own story. What are you going to do, Joseph said, now that you're out, what are your plans, where are you going to live? Edward stopped walking, he jumped onto a rotting log lying at the side of the path, Oh, I've got a plan, I've got a job but it won't pay for a while, right now I need some money. So that's what it's about, thought Joseph, extortion pure and simple, actually not extortion but straight-out blackmail if it involves a threat to Alison. About this he kept silent for fear of putting ideas into Edward's head though he knew the idea must be there already along with countless others most likely. Guess what the most valuable thing you can have in prison is, demanded Edward from atop the log, I bet you can't. Joseph shrugged, what did he know, he couldn't think where to start. Give up, he said. Flipflops. It's true, you reckon they have carpets in there, your feet get freezing, then there's the showers, people shit in them because they're too lazy to do it in the proper place or because the doors have been taken off the toilets, there's blood in them, the showers, there's sperm in them, hair every-where. Edward, I just need to talk to you about what you're going to do now. Down upon his father gazed the son, perhaps it was the yellow light through shifting leaves that created the illusion of a tremor on his lower lip and chin, twenty-three hours a day lockdown! Edward yelled. Come down from there, Joseph said, not quite

73

pleading, let's go back to the van. The idea of a soothing walk in the woods was not working out so well, he knew his son lived in a world of vivid imagination, the buried mannikin being a case in point, now he wondered if the space and splendour of the woodland, as he saw it, might be clashing or interacting in some unfortunate way with Edward's memories of long imprisonment. Conjecture for sure though perhaps not so far from the truth. And then, remember, hadn't he been warned in one of the clinics, one of the many white rooms where seven years ago he'd first encountered those words like disengagement, disassociation, disruption, delusion, the last one, delusion, being the most important, supposedly it provided the key, not that a key was really any use when you came right down to it, it might offer an explanation but zero in the way of actual understanding, zero in the way of consolation, it was a name and nothing more when all was said and done, hadn't he been warned back then that Edward might at times suffer from an overload of sensory input, that it might be an associated symptom. What do you mean? he'd asked. Just too much information coming in, the clinician told him, too much activity, too much noise, too many smells, imagine Clapham Junction with the same number of trains arriving but there's only one platform open, they're all trying to use that one platform, the analogy was good, straightaway Joseph got the picture. Never had it occurred to him that Barrows Wood might be a location for overload. But then again nature could be aggravating at the best of times, all that walking, nowhere to buy a drink, the turds of animals underfoot, insects biting, nettles stinging when the need to relieve oneself becomes overwhelming, it's not everyone's cup of tea, nature never really speaks to us anyway, if it did we'd run a mile, thank heavens for concrete and our addiction to it. Besides which, although Joseph's headache was softening, the plaster on his lacerated thumb needed replacing again and there weren't any in his pockets, he must have shoved them in the glove compartment, how tedious, truly if it isn't one thing it's the other.

The two of them made their way back to the plumber's van, what an expedition it had been, less than half a mile travelled in old money. But Edward seemed happier, his composure was restored, a break in the circuit, a spark gone rogue, that's all the shouting on top of the log had been, he even gave the impression of believing that he'd acted humorously. When was the last time he ate, Joseph wondered as he rummaged in the glove compartment, as he peeled and applied a new plaster to his thumb. I'll buy him some food, we'll go in search of it now, a full stomach always puts a person in a better mood. How about it? Edward nodded, Yes, sounds good, but first he wanted to show his father something. From behind the passenger headrest where he'd left it hanging he pulled the fashionable-enough bag, the satchel-thing made of canvas, only when Edward placed it in his lap did Joseph understand there to be something of weight inside, what, suddenly he wasn't sure he wanted to know, he'd had enough surprises for one day, sometimes it's better to remain ignorant. It's to do with my new job, Edward said, it's quite something, *this* is quite something, don't think I'm just going to drift now that I'm out, take a look. He opened the buckles, one, two, how stylish, from the canvas bag he took an object wrapped in strips torn from a piece of bedding, cotton, clean, he passed it across to Joseph, Unwrap it, this is my starter. The thing had heft. Joseph unwrapped it, under the rags was a knife, the most extraordinarily vicious knife he'd ever seen, at once he was astonished, at once he was frightened, what message was Edward sending him, should he open the door and fling it as far from the van as possible, should he call the police, should he have done that the moment he saw Edward standing in Amanda Margaret's doorway rather than inviting him into the van, what a mistake, should he simply run for his life, or for hers, Alison's, did this mean he was going to try to kill her again? Edward laughed seeing the effect it had, Ha ha, an ungenerous laugh, sly, always there'd been this side to him that Joseph couldn't read, he couldn't read it now, something permanently veiled. You're just carrying this around? he cried out. Magnificent, isn't it, pick it up, there's history there, real history. No said Joseph, he started re-wrapping the knife in the rags, what an unwieldy thing, not to mention dangerous, three long blades that bulged and curved like fleurs-de-lys, a dark knobbled handle made from God knows what, if he touched it he'd leave fingerprints, blood even, from his thumb, paranoid thought but it felt justified, he wanted the thing out of his sight, could anything be less of a token of reconciliation than this, what was Edward trying to do to him?

Diego gave it to me, his son said, taking the knife and holding it up, turning it in his fingers with theatrical admiration. It's worth a bit, to a collector. Who's Diego? Not everyone you meet inside is a thug, not everyone in there is a moron, we got along, we hit it off, someone interesting to talk to, you know, on the same wing as me. Edward laid the knife in his lap, he pulled the rags around it, he cocooned it and tied the strips back in place. Well, this is what he does, arms and armour, the antique stuff, makes a fortune, he was there to pick me up when I got out and that was something too, he drives a Bentley. What was he in for? Dodgy taxes. That's all? That's all. Must've been a lot. I didn't ask, first thing you learn is not to pry. Joseph didn't like the sound of this at all, who was this Diego, who was he to get involved? But then looking at matters objectively, and it was important to always try to do that, how much had he, Joseph, been involved? He hadn't visited, he hadn't written, he'd thought about Edward all the time but confusedly, he hadn't wanted to pick sides but still it had happened, time and Alison had seen to that. So what was he to Edward now? Very little. Perhaps nothing, seven years was a long time. No right to feel resentful. And what was Diego? He was more, he was something. Diego, Joseph said, what kind of a—? Don't worry, he's lived in England all his life, that's just his name. He's older than me, actually I think he's older than *you*. And how much does something like that go for? said Joseph, indicating the knife in its wrapping. A fair bit, to the right buyer, a collector, this one will go to an Arab probably, from Dubai or Saudi, do you want to hear about it, the knife, I mean? Cautiously Joseph nodded and Edward told him its history, the provenance he called it, everything was documented, that was of the greatest importance, the authentication, it came from Africa, the knobbled covering on the handle was crocodile skin, crocodile from the White Nile. Once the knife belonged to a follower of the Mahdi, sometimes called the mad Mahdi, used in the siege of Khartoum, the death of General Gordon 1885, hazily Joseph remembered the name, Gordon, Gordon, so many generals had gone out from these islands, thousands of them, he wondered what this one had been doing in Khartoum, wherever that was. The stuff Diego has said Edward, he was becoming enthusiastic, not just Victorian stuff, American Civil War, Napoleonic, Chinese, Japanese, he even has a cannon from the Battle of Waterloo, I've seen it, this is a gift, it's not really worth that much, not comparatively, but what it is, you see, he wants me to go in with him, learn the trade, take over when he retires. Edward paused for effect, truly this was news, a career, international travel, wealthy contacts, not many emerge from prison with such bright prospects. Joseph stayed silent. It's just that I need a suit, Edward continued, he was trying to catch his father's eye now, fix him with a meaningful look, a phone, new shoes, you have to look the part for these Arabs and Americans, they're high rollers, it's a prestige thing. Can't Diego help with that? He's already done enough said Edward, he's not my father.

If he got it, this money, some amount of money, would that be it, would he go away and never come near his parents again, or would it be the first of many payments, blackmails, money here, money there, the threat to Alison present but always unspoken? Inconclusive scenarios played out in Joseph's mind, the only commonality to them was that his feelings came last in every one, they dropped through the cracks, they were lost, unimportant. Alison had to be protected, Edward dealt with, how cunning was the boy being, how simple, it needed consideration, more hurt was on the way for sure. Though he had to admit – going from poisoning to weaponry was sort of logical.

9

From outside, the coffeeshop looked like an Alpine chalet, timbered gable-ends and a little white clock tower. There were better places to eat than here but the man Joseph had found himself driving this way unconsciously, the feeder roads guiding him without blockage across roundabout and past petrol station, in front of an SUV showroom decked with hangings of rugged empty landscapes, pleasantly then to be conducted inside the perimeter of the retail park where ahead reclined both superstore and the coffeeshop which was its most exciting zone. Other than neatly clipped banks of foliage once green but now droughted a more perfectly organised slice of heaven could not be conceived. Joseph slid into a bay close to the coffeeshop, even the parking was convenient, free for up to two hours and he thought it unlikely they'd need more time than that. There's a cashpoint said Edward, pointing to a place beneath the superstore's generous eaves, two in fact. Joseph cut the engine then saw his son shouldering the canvas bag. I'm not going in there with you if you're carrying that thing. Why not? I'm just not, that's all. The Mahdi's knife wasn't something to be taken into public places, what if Edward decided to unwrap it again, it looked so brutal, a weapon for a beheading, it might provoke trouble of the most serious kind, images of armed response units played in Joseph's head. Edward shrugged, it didn't matter to him, he hooked the strap over the headrest and pushed the bag once more behind the passenger seat then without further prompting left the van and joined the small queue waiting for use of the bank machines. What a nerve! The brass neck! Joseph swept past him, was that what they learned in prison, he'd told his son he would buy him something to eat, a meal, whatever substantial thing they had on the menu, no agreement whatsoever had been reached about cash being handed over. If money *was* to be involved certain conditions would have to be attached, what those might be Joseph didn't yet know, he was still unsure whether or not to believe Edward's story of Diego, this man older than Joseph himself, the trade in antique arms and armour, the hobnobbing with wealthy Arabs and Americans, could it be true, well why not, it sounded possible and impossible at the same time. How unsettling not to have more clues. From a young age Edward had possessed talents for deception, for pulling the wool as it's antiquarianly called, yet if in reality it was all a pack of lies the question then arose, where had the knife come from? For you did not have to be an authority on such matters to know with cast-iron certainty that it was an object both foreign and archaic.

Inside the coffeeshop the Alpine theme gave way to the Mediterranean, wall-sized images of happy Italians, how

well dressed they were, how carefree, it must be the inges-
tion of all that olive oil. Unfortunately it could not be said
that the clientele then present, sparse at this time of day,
displayed the same effortless sophistication. Some of their
clothes had the look of hand-me-downs, to their bodies
clung a distinct lumberingness as if elegance having tiptoed
close once had declined to linger. Sunburns were slabbily
on view and foreheads had acquired a hue similar to the
postboxes so beloved in these islands. Edward meanwhile
slouched in unembarrassed by the rebuff outside. The
pair ordered food, they took their seats, it was a booth,
nice and private, Edward picking a spot that faced the
door and car park. Sulkily enough he sat, silence can be
a weapon too, embarrass the other person into speaking
first. But who cared about that, Joseph didn't, now he was
thinking along altogether different lines, how fast our minds
swerve, his default position had been to assume Edward
was lying, that Edward had returned as a harbinger of
doom, some thought-image like that, but perhaps instead
he was about to fly for good into the arms of Diego, the
Arabs and Americans, never to be seen or heard of again.
After all what did Joseph have to offer, nothing, he'd sided
with Alison. This might in actual reality be the last time
he'd ever see his son. If you want me to give you money,
Joseph said, in how many endless ways had he imagined
this scene but never like this, any money at all, you'll have
to answer my questions, straight answers I mean. Shoot
said Edward. Why did you try to poison Alison? I didn't
try to poison her, I *did* poison her. Joseph slammed his
hands down on the table, how foolish, now the cut to his
thumb would probably start bleeding when it had only

just stopped. His ears roared, suddenly in the privacy of the booth he was a heartbeat away from taking his son by the throat and choking the life out of him, the little bastard deserved all he got. You're still under her influence, aren't you said Edward. How stupid to think there could be that sort of reconciliation, or any reconciliation at all! But then the boy had something wrong in his head, didn't he, some tiny part of it that worked fine for everybody else, that connected for everybody else, but not for him, it wasn't his fault and Joseph had to keep reminding himself of that because it distracted from those parts of his own insides which a moment before had been smooth and unnoticed but which now were unmeshing and fighting. Whirlpoolishly they teemed, Joseph wrestled to get them under control, to get himself under control. Here you are said the waitress, she smiled, she bent down, one plate, a second plate, she brought across salt and pepper from another table, they say it's going to be cooler tomorrow, let's hope so, enjoy your meal. Thank you said Edward. Thank you said Joseph. Placidly the waitress returned to her station behind the counter. It is not necessary to describe the food she brought, it was sufficient. You tried to kill your own mother, Joseph said. And I've done the time for it, replied Edward, I've paid my debt to society, three times I went before the parole board, the last time they were unanimous, I'm no longer deemed to be a risk, he smiled at the very idea. I never was anyway, not to society at large, not to the *general public*, they always knew that. They should've warned me, Joseph said, they should've let me know. Edward shrugged his shoulders, such administrative details were of little concern to him.

So you're out on licence? I'm out, I'm free. You can't go anywhere near her, Edward. I don't want to, I've no intention of doing that. Is it, why are you here then, you can't go within a mile of the house, the banning order is permanent, I don't know anything about your release, what the details are, but I know that. Now Joseph was in full flow. You can't contact her in any way, you can't email her, you can't send anything through the post. I don't have anything to send and I couldn't afford the postage even if I did said Edward. You've got that knife, try sending that and your feet won't touch the ground, I'll make sure of it personally.

A woman stood at the end of their table holding in her open palms bundles of spinous plant matter tied about with ribbons. Lucky heather, lucky heather, she said. By her side a young girl clutched a teddy bear. The girl wore a dirty yellow cardigan and the woman a black shawl, both their faces needed a wash, the woman's English was bad and her accent strange and when she said anything other than lucky heather the words were impossible for Joseph to understand. Perhaps this mother and child have stepped out of the back alleys behind the apartments where the well-dressed and carefree Italians live, for the truth is they don't belong here, they're beggars, and if the Alpine-Mediterranean coffeeshop had been busier and the waitress not momentarily vanished from behind the counter they would have found themselves chased off in a minute. Lucky heather, lucky heather grunted the woman waving her spinous bundles at father and son. Joseph was fully aware of the old superstition, if you refuse to buy heather from a gypsy she'll put a curse on you, in his place Amanda Margaret Hollander would have purchased the lot knowing correctly that white heather is the most talismanic variety of that species, but what time did Joseph have for this, he waved her away, so what if a curse fell on him, he was maxed out on bad luck already. The girl in the dirty yellow cardigan stared at him, her eyes were big and blank, she seized hold of a greasy shawl-end and followed her mother to the next table. Does Diego know about your diagnosis, Joseph asked, that's what I'd like to know. It's none of his business. But he must have asked why you were in, wherever it was you met him. Kirkham, I met him at Kirkham – it's an open prison – and yes he did ask but only once, I made something up and he didn't ask again, you don't do that. Joseph forked and swallowed a mouthful of food, he didn't know what an open prison was, it sounded like a funny thing for a prison to be, did the inmates wander in and out whenever they felt like it, was it a sort of farm, a labour camp, then he remembered such places weren't allowed any more, only in countries like North Korea, you imagined some peasant putting down his hoe in the heat of the day and in the minute of taking an illegal breather being ripped to pieces by attack dogs of the regime, could it really be like that? Capgras no longer plays a part in my life, Edward said. In fact I've followed the research and I believe it may have been a misdiagnosis. Followed the research? Joseph was surprised, once he'd tried himself to read some of the psychiatric stuff, it wouldn't stay in his head, he kept reading the same page over and over. How could you, where you've been? I got in touch with a charity, Edward said, I wrote to them, they send things like that into prisons for free, very specific books or magazines if they think they have educational value, if it'll help someone rehabilitate, that's always a good word to use when you ask, rehabilitation, then there are others, people who just have a thing about it, you know, sending books to prisoners, you can tap into that, anyway I got hold of the stuff, the screws tried to stop it but I appealed, in the end they don't care, they're trapped in there and hating it like everyone else. Well psychiatry's like everything else, it has fashions, Capgras syndrome was in one category, now it's in another, everything's a category, *you're* a category Dad, those who suffer from it only really pose a danger to themselves, not even a danger in fact, not even a problem, it's just something to be aware of, things have changed, that's what my solicitor told the parole board. Those other people who have it didn't do what you did said Joseph, trying to be calm. Just because the name for something's changed it doesn't mean you've changed, if you had I could ask you one question, right now, who is Alison, and you'd give a simple answer, you'd say, Alison is my mother, look, I'm not asking you to love her, I know you can't do that, I'm asking you to acknowledge the fact, the very basic fact, that Alison gave birth to you, she brought you up, the woman is your mother, nobody else is, it's her. Alison is an imposter, Edward said.

So much for a misdiagnosis. You didn't put a foot wrong in there, did you? The man Joseph didn't bother trying to keep the bitterness out of his voice, he knew no way of

86

dealing with this, reasoning wasn't working, anger wasn't working, neither was pleading, one day he'd let everything out with a scream, or a howl, how gargantuan it would be, how wild, but not here, the boy was still his son, you can't go around howling in coffeeshops anyway, he needed to be practical. No doubt the parole board, the committee, the decision-makers, were clever people, eminent, no doubt they had behind them qualifications, years of experience, yet sitting in this Alpine-Mediterranean coffeeshop it discomforted Joseph to know that his family had been the subject of their intimate and detailed discussions, The restraining order carries some weight, we mustn't forget that, keep one mile away from the family home at all times or wherever the mother Alison Forbes happens to be, don't make contact with her of any kind, Yes, I think we can rely on that, after all he's never shown the least indication of being a threat to anyone else, we've all read the reports, In my opinion he shouldn't even be in an ordinary jail, Yes, I agree, We all agree, And it's obvious to me at least that he's tried his best since being with us, look at the privileges he's earned... and neither, thought Joseph, neither could it be denied that Edward had a certain charisma, no not that exactly, difficult thing to put a word to, but something intangible that he could touch people with if he chose to, if he was in the mood to. It was easy in any case to imagine the members of the parole board agonising over his case file only to rubberstamp approval at the end of long deliberations.

There are blokes in there who'll never get out, Edward was saying, once there was a riot, the whole wing went

87

up, I stayed out of it, well away from it, what loyalty do I have to them, five or six years they got on top of what they were already doing, you have to be able to say sorry, show some remorse but these blokes can't bear to, they're too proud, they don't see it's a game, I worked that out pretty quick. Remorse! cried Joseph, saying sorry! Give me some money and I'll go away, Edward said. What a formulation for a father to hear and a son to say. Joseph stood up, he could not push his chair back because this was a booth, between the table and padded seat he eased himself, Wait here. As he left the coffeeshop the Mediterranean dropped away though the sun above the car park continued to boil, to him action now seemed essential, it was not commonly his style to sit around all day talking, there were limits to how much could be achieved by long discussion, not much was his experience, towards those who spent the hours of their lives discoursing he held a measure of contempt never displayed on those rare occasions he happened to meet them but held inalienably close to his heart or wherever such convictions might be kept. These people had to realise a simple fact, that it was men like him, like Joseph, who kept the world turning, who repaired their plumbing, emptied their bins, refined their oil, grew and packed their foodstuffs, filled in potholes, debugged their computers, delivered their mail order items, dug their graves, without them and their efforts commerce as it is generally recognised would grind to a halt and the discoursing would be over and ended. Such people added little to the world in his view. And the grey-haired and crone-handed old lady who was the single other person queuing for use of the bank machines must have agreed because quietly as she waited, reading the Daily Mail, she tut-tutted, yes, the world was indeed tut-worthy.

How much to give? From the deep pockets of his work-trousers he fished his wallet, he ought to get more plasters while he was here too, at the superstore, tomorrow I'll be back at Amanda's finishing off the cylinder job. At the screen when his turn came he tapped in the first numbers. Joseph's wallet held cards to three current accounts, each had a domestic appellation agreed informally between himself and Alison, we shan't trouble the reader with the names, those who share or have shared their money can easily imagine. The balances looked good, he was surprised, but then Alison was doing well at work, she spent very little money, in recent months he'd spent almost none, how much to give? Money was money, it was precious, a quantum to be watched, for some it came easily but not for Joseph, never for Joseph. And this money had been earned by Alison, Alison who'd supported him when the breakdown came and when it stayed, so what right did he have to go helping himself? But once Edward had been a blob easing itself in milli-metres from between her thighs and he'd watched, he'd held the blob, he'd even cut the cord for God's sake – now a grown man with his own history, an unpleasant history for sure, all the same you couldn't deny biology. Inexpressible horror that this might be the last time of meeting, what it would mean in the reality of unfolding years. And a sense of unfairness because not all fathers looked upon their offspring like this, some couldn't wait to see the back of them, why did he have to be one of those that cared? Each account had a maximum withdrawal limit of £250, from each he took that amount, he would worry about explaining it later, the cash appeared from the mechanical slot, he took and folded it, no need to count it because these automatic teller machines never cheat, unlike people they can be relied upon every time. Then he walked back into the coffeeshop and silently handed the money over to his son, Diego's son now it seemed, whoever Diego was. The thought chilled him, nobody ever got their due in life, you went through a period of bad fortune then believed you were owed a period of good, that was what he'd thought this morning when he'd watched Amanda Margaret Hollander bob about the kitchen with her blouse straining open at the third button, how misguided, how foolish, things don't work like that, they don't balance up, you shouldn't have an expectation they ever will, yet always you did. Thank you said Edward, stowing the cash inside his clothing, polishing his glasses with a shirt corner and replacing them. I'll pay you back.

The coffeeshop's anti-annihilation device in the meantime had ticked almost to four, both it and the superstore were filling up with those wishing to purchase their after-work supplies. If the weather stayed like this the weekend would be good for outdoor eating, how considerate it was of the local managers to ensure that the barbecue aisle was fully stocked. But now that Edward had finished his meal and received his payoff, sad to call it that, Joseph wondered, What next? He considered it likely the boy, he wasn't a boy, would ask for a lift somewhere. Near, far? Far would be good, conducive to easy sleeping later on, plus he might pick up more information on a long ride. Is that God-botherer still hanging around? Edward asked. Colleen, no, she's gone. I read a bit of it myself, you know, inside, the Bible, got to be pretty familiar with it. Alison gets a lot of comfort from that book, she's become quite serious about— Why did you do it interrupted Edward, and something in his voice made Joseph look at him anew. He had not particularly been avoiding his son's gaze but now in the sun-filled coffeeshop he saw the fierce set of Edward's mouth and the deadly seriousness in his eyes, Why did you call the police, why did you side with her, that bitch, that imposter, we could have come to an arrangement, we could have left and gone somewhere, lived on our own... In the depths of Edward's voice tears were accumulating and some quality or angle of the light was causing him to look paler all of a sudden. This is insane, Joseph told him, I *saw you* come out myself, how many more times do I have to tell you, I was there, at the birth, Alison is your mother, she's your mother. For a long moment Edward stared out of the window, then he stood up. Good old Dad, he said maliciously, good old Joseph, good old Daddikins, he raised his elbows in front of his face and hunched his back, was I cute, was I all curled up like this? Course you were, that's how they come out – babies. Well, thanks for the money, I'm just... Edward nodded to an alcove near the entrance of the coffeeshop, a stuccoed recess that led to the toilets, he passed a Tuscan citadel, he disappeared.

During this conversation Joseph had been sitting with his back to the glass doors of the coffeeshop, his son Edward, despite the enclosing privacy of the booth, facing the doors with a view of the superstore's atrium and car park beyond. Now from this direction came a disturbance, a ripple, an unsettlement, heads turned, something was happening. Two policemen in shirtsleeves order had entered the premises while on the hot tarmacadam outside a second pair stood newly stationed. No, Sorry, Only just got here, I'll keep a eye out, these were the replies Joseph heard in response to the shirtsleeved officers' inquiries, then catching the word heather he understood the policemen were looking for the woman with the greasy shawl and the child in the dirty yellow cardigan. Someone had alerted the authorities, these beggars really were a nuisance, if they were foreign and certainly they seemed to be, might it not be possible to deport them? Woe betide the individual who made the call however, for not once in a hundred lifetimes will they receive the luck of the white heather. One of the policemen approached Joseph. Have you seen, they were here, often they use children, they operate in rings, the policeman's nose was sunburned, he carried a bottle of water, the camera attached to his black protective vest recorded this and every other humdrum encounter, when would he become a detective, a yawn threatened but he suppressed it, it was important to remain professional in all dealings with the public. What? said Joseph, no, no, I don't remember anything like that, a shrug, he pretended ignorance, already the policeman was walking off, at the door he spoke into his radio, from its loudspeaker a central voice issued new instructions and presently the pair strode away.

Fifteen minutes went by. Twenty. No Edward. Past the Tuscan citadel the man Joseph went, he entered and checked the men's toilets, empty, knocking on the door of the women's toilets and hearing nothing he boldly put his head inside, empty but a window open, a window pushed down. Out in the car park the policemen were interacting lightheartedly with shoppers. Joseph walked to the van and sat behind the wheel, the air was stifling, he rolled down the driver's window, around him the world was lively, customers, deliveries, the outflow and inflow of goods, all the good people like him who kept the world turning, still hanging behind the headrest of the passenger seat was the canvas bag containing the Mahdi's knife.

10

Silent, still, quivering inside, it was a nice kind of quivering, the kind that fills you up, the woman Alison Forbes waited upon a soft-seated chair in the cool of the travel agency. Open on her lap was a brochure, the pictures digitally enhanced she knew, taken early in the morning before the crowds arrived, that's how it works, in car adverts you never see other cars, in holiday brochures you never see tourists, the footworn paths of the planet must be given a lonely and adventuresome appearance if the customer is to be parted successfully from their money. Over our narrative Alison's hovered, a cloud in the sky, a charge in the atmosphere, for a time we wondered if she would arrive at all, now in this old-fashioned office the moment's here and the first thing we notice about her is the bristling forearm hairs which might be stirring in reaction to the large electric fan that's sweeping the room with cooler air or might, alternatively, be responding to this inside-quivering. In any case we may be sure the exotic places depicted in her travel brochure have some part of it, they've got her full attention. There's hardly anyone else in the travel agency right now, they're all too busy being on holiday to book a holiday, if only they'd known about the heatwave maybe they wouldn't have bothered, yet despite choosing the timing of her visit well Alison still has to wait, office work, admin, is keeping the travel agents busy. But that's OK, it's good to be alive, to feel this artificial breeze on your arms, to consider the temples and basilicas, the colourful rock formations and anciently ruined walls and the decision they present her with, a decision which in truth is only a shield for the larger decision she realises she's going to have to make, sooner, later, sometime, never.

One particular line in the brochure she pondered. If you select to share a twin room when booking but have no-one to share with we will try to pair you up with someone of the same gender in the group. About this she wanted to ask, the single room supplement was £399, ever such a lot, the holiday, the trip, she dared hardly utter the other word, pilgrimage, even to herself, was expensive enough as it was. Well, she was only here to make enquiries, find things out in general, no decision had been made yet, no detailed budgeting done. But she wished Joe would message her. In his direction she sent a stream of good wishes, not vocal prayers because they were something else but a pulsation of blessings, out of the door of the travel agent's they flew, across town to the house where she knew he was working and then in at whichever aperture they might best be received into his soul, which was everlasting. Today was quite the milestone and she hoped it was going well for him. Of course Joe *coming along* was out of the question, a trip like this would be wasted on him, he wouldn't scoff exactly, in all likelihood he'd say nothing, but the lack of connection would ruin it for her, she'd feel constantly the need to justify and explain when all she wanted to do was go quietly from place to place and – well, she didn't know exactly. Bathe in the atmosphere, she supposed, breathe it in, touch the relics and rocks, feel the textures, taste the dust, all those who'd walked there before, where He had walked, where He had laid His hands, immerse herself somehow in the lives of those others who would also be present, the thousands, open herself up to a sort of emptying and refilling, a smile, what was she, a petrol pump, oh it was hard, it was impossible to explain for any number of reasons! If only Colleen could go with her – but she was seeing Colleen tonight and that was enough. How can I help you? asked the travel agent. He was free now. He beckoned her over with his eyes and gave a wave, Sorry to keep you waiting, this heat is scrambling my brain a little. Yes it is a bit much isn't it, Alison replied. What a pleasant way to start the conversation, where would we be without the ever-changing moods of the weather to comment upon. I was only here to make an enquiry really, across the desk she handed the brochure, the travel agent took it, he glanced at it, he was young with a beard, back in the day with Amanda Margaret Hollander no young man they'd been acquainted with would have been seen dead with a beard, then came the thought that perhaps it was a sign but no that was ridiculous, if a beard could be a sign then anything could be a sign, now you're looking for excuses. She pointed at the brochure, I wanted to know if I could book onto this with you, or anything like it, I wanted to ask about the single room supplement too. What dates did you have in mind? Easter, Easter really. Let me see said the agent, placing the brochure beside his computer. Easter next year? Alison nodded, yes obviously next year she thought but didn't say, the young man tapped at the keyboard, he examined and analysed the flow of information called forth, how different to the way they must have done it in olden times, the caravans of monks and knights and donkeys overland across Europe, half-starved most of the time, I'd like to read some of those accounts, there's no end of things to read now. Easter is the most expensive time to go said the young man. Yes, I thought it might be… The cool air from the electric fan swept again over her bare forearms, it clutched at the pages of the brochure, Colleen said it had been marvellous. I can get you four nights in Jerusalem and two in Galilee, the young man told her, he read aloud dates and prices, it was expensive but not outrageously so. And here's another one, with this you get a night in Tel Aviv to sample the nightlife. I'm not really interested in the nightlife, I'm getting a bit old for that now. Behind his beard Alison saw the young man smile, but nicely, she smiled too, I'm more interested in the Church of the Holy Sepulchre these days, she said. Well who isn't, answered the young man and they both laughed. Look the system's being slow today, would you mind if I just grab a coffee, he nodded over his shoulder to a door marked Employees Only, it'll only take a second, we have a machine back there. No problem said Alison. Clever of him, introducing this light note of complicity, he probably sells lots of holidays, often it must come down to that element of almost wanting someone else to make the decision for you. Now if only Joe would send her a message, text her, Everything fine, C u later x, that would be enough, it would free up some space in her mind. But the reality was she had no serious concerns, moreover she was playing at booking this trip, daydreaming through a lunch hour, killing time till tonight. Almost thirty the girl must be now! Of course she hadn't told Joe about Colleen being at the meeting, about her being the main speaker in fact. The dates had fallen badly in the end but there was no getting around that and definitely no point in getting him worked up all over again. How lucky she'd been to meet her, how unthinkable that they might have missed each other. But there she'd been, hesitant, tentative, yes those were the two words that described her best in those early days – poking her head round the bunched-up hospital curtain after it was pulled back. Easily retrieved image. The black hair misty at the ends, pimple on the chin, the long russet shirt like a smock, Hello, I'm a visitor, I'm going around, if you'd like someone to talk to…? Oh – hello, yes, OK, why not, for a couple of minutes anyway, before I get too tired. The haemodialysis had finished, they'd checked her blood pressure, they'd checked her temperature, her heart rate, everything that could be checked had been checked, all within acceptable parameters, her kidneys were on the mend, it had been touch and go and everyone knew it, the doctors were pleased, they were delighted. This was in the months before the trial came crawling and sliming over the protective boundaries, never say his name again. Not His name, because that contains all, but *his* name. So the girl came into the cubicle, she sat on the visitor's chair, they talked, pleasantries at first. With a name like that you must be Irish. French said Colleen. Somehow the accents had sounded similar. Would you be interested in taking one of these? She held out a booklet shaped like a bus timetable, it was Matthew, Oh she's *that* sort of visitor Alison thought, well that's fine, I suppose, there's the Cross on her necklace, didn't see it before. And so pretty – image of the daughter she'd always wanted. That was the emotional core of it, the hypnotic start. Then the next day when she'd visited at Alison's request, with Alison waiting for her, that was strange too because her intention had been to let the girl do the talking, to listen to her and watch her, it would be soothing and didn't she need some soothing after the treatment she'd had, black and blue and wretched the haemodialysis left you, the needles they put in, the tubes into the neck, the back of the hand, being hooked up and washed out by that humming block of machinery, the dressings afterwards, the headaches, the nausea, what kind of life was this, never had the sentiment what doesn't kill you makes you stronger felt more of a lie. Yet instead of listening it was her, Alison, who'd started talking, first about the haemo, and certainly she'd had to get that out, then about the husband who now that the immediate crisis was past was not spending quite so much time at the hospital, he had his business to run of course and in that line of work you couldn't afford to stand still for a moment, and finally, finally, was it possible that she'd said it out loud to a stranger (but already she trusted Colleen), the worst thing, the most awful thing, terrible, terrible, horrific, how can I ever come to terms with it when it was done *on purpose*, her own – the son – she'd given birth to had done it *deliberately*. The pouring of antifreeze into her drink. It didn't hurt, not at first, it was even funny, they thought I was drunk, staggering about, slurring, he'd got impatient you see and poured in too much, sweetener he called it, you always had a sweet tooth Mum, I remember him saying, you've always liked your tea that way, if he'd stuck to his plan I wouldn't be here talking to you now. Lying then in the hospital ward she'd sobbed, she didn't care who else heard, the tears fell like drool past her ears and onto the place in her neck where the dialysis tube had so recently been removed, the dressing pinked wetly, the girl called Colleen gazed down into her lap where the fingers of her hands rested interlocked and upward palmed, she'd come here expecting to talk about God or Jesus, really there was no difference although actually there very much was and that was what she was trying to get to the bottom of and what the training was for, this visiting of hospitals being one part of that training, a way of showing commitment, and while she was used to people turning her away, sometimes quite rudely, there was no way she was used to this or possessed anywhere near the experience or emotional capacity to deal with it – not even fluent in English yet. Knowing only as the words came out between tears and sobs which lessened gradually that she mustn't run away from this poor woman lying on the bed before her, that this encounter was a part of her education, a part of

God's plan. Meanwhile in the story which was the story of her illness the woman Alison had collapsed, she couldn't stand, she was gagging, the ambulance had been called, 999, in France it was 18 or 15, a terrible scene was taking place between the husband of this woman and the son, a bottle of something being waved about, the two were shouting, they were fighting, sirens, police, to open up like this to a stranger – but people were extraordinary, they pretended everything was fine and lived in such secret pain, they had to be cherished, at the bottom of it all so much fragile innocence. And then the drug they'd pumped into her, Alison Forbes, yes that was her name, the antidote supposedly, had nearly killed her, five days she'd been in a coma. Well that's it, if you're in a coma it's over, goodnight Vienna, that's what people think isn't it? Colleen couldn't understand what the capital of Austria had to do with it but she got the point, she got the sense, she listened when Alison told her of the spiked crystals that had contaminated her blood, they were the poison, they were the work of the Devil, when Collen heard that word she shuddered inside knowing for sure this meeting was no accident. The crystals were what had to be dealt with, you couldn't just pee them out, well somehow she'd got through it, she'd lived, she'd lived, but it took a long time to understand what had happened, the full implications. And then, Alison said smiling grimly, then it was just a simple matter of dealing with the kidney failure.

Was that how it had been, either for her or for Colleen? Even now Alison couldn't be certain. Hospitals had such an air of unreality about them, time moved differently there, she'd been so ill, so upset, her mind blowing in every direction, the world itself heaped in grey ramparts, vaporous somehow, confusing, they penned her in. But that was how she remembered it anyway, that was the substance of what had happened and been said. All touring and transfers by air-conditioned coach as per the itinerary said the travel agent, he was returning with his coffee, sitting down, with him he had a sheaf of printouts, flight schedules, visa requirements, how helpful he was, how helpful everyone was really, even Joe most of the time. Though another truth and one she didn't so much like admitting to herself was that the space her husband occupied in her head, if such space signified his importance, was scaling down, smaller now than it had been even one month ago. Yes, we can book you onto this, flights are with British Airways, arrival at Tel Aviv Ben Gurion airport said the young man who then began to read out loud details of the Holy Land. Colleen almost thirty. But it was that mention of the Devil that hooked her in the first time, yes I'm certain of it, that's what got her interested. What else had she said in delirium? Around him in these nightmares of mine people crawl, they burn, that phrase presented itself to her mind, surely not, how melodramatic, but oh Colleen turned white when I said it. Possibly I did lay it on a bit thick there. Well she *asked* so I *told* her. Not so melodramatic after all. Please come again, I said – must have begged her to, looking back, and what she heard at the trial only confirmed it, everything that came out, the mannikin Joe burned, the altar in the woods, no proof of the cat but a few went missing round that time and I wouldn't put it past him. Capgras syndrome *my backside.* Nothing but psychobabble. Devil, or willingly of the Devil's side. Demon. How much clearer could it be, it's *in Scripture.* And forget, for the last time forget, what happened with the bus, don't torment yourself with that any more, he was so little then it can't possibly have made a difference, it can't. So, what would you like to do? asked the travel agent. I'm – oh, sorry, I was – miles away, how rude of me, could you say that again? The young man took a sip of coffee, he stroked his beard, in this heat it was bothersome, it itched, perhaps he should shave it off, no, the sad truth was the beard got more attention than he did, without the beard girls would never talk to him. He knew this woman wasn't going to book any holiday. No deposit would be forthcoming. It didn't take long to learn the types, though not many came in asking about the Holy Land. Most likely she was on a late lunchbreak, indulging a dream, dreams were what they sold after all and she did look like she could use a holiday, not just the sun, there was enough of that at the moment, but a break, a proper break, get away from it all. Still, no money, no dice. Would you like to go away and think about it, you can take these with you, kindly he offered the print-outs, what need was there to embarrass her, hadn't they laughed together about the Church of the Holy Sepulchre? Thank you, I think I'll do that, it was only a general enquiry as I said, sort of spontaneous, I don't want to take up your time. Hardly spontaneous when daily she imagined following the Via Dolorosa or climbing the Mount of Beatitudes. And daily Mount and road hit the hard-stopping fact of Joe. But she'd get there one year, you see if she wouldn't.

All at once the woman Alison felt weary, overcome, she needed to get outside, into the air, a change of scenery, she wasn't as much of a rock these days as she liked to think. Not a problem said the travel agent, that's what I'm here for, his words seemed genuine but he can't really mean he's here to have his time wasted by silly middle-aged women like me thought Alison. Weakly she smiled, she pushed open the glass door of the travel agency and stepped onto the heat of the pavement, into the light of the street, where were her sunglasses, she fumbled in her bag, I got totally distracted just then, let those things be forgotten, don't try to haul them back, there's no need to be a memory-fisher now that He's come alive for me, the truth of His Resurrection, for surely if there's a Devil there's Christ on the opposite side, I know there is. Along the street she walked, stop here then in the shade of this boarded-up shop and try, really try for that quivering emptying feeling, fleetingly I had it earlier, I had it, where did it go. For I fear, lest, when I come, I shall not find you such as I would. But that's the mistake, isn't it, to go looking in the first place, I never found Him, He found me, oh if only I could bring Joe inside, if only he'd open up instead of living forever in that dreamworld of his, ignorant, inconsequential. Today ought to do him good though, get him back into circulation, maybe he'll go to the pub afterwards, a pint or two, talk about football or women, anything, politics even, that's how it should be with men instead of this moping around, I know I'm not being fair, he's been so ill, nervous breakdowns aren't small things, you don't get over them in three days, four weeks he went without getting out of bed, staring at the wall, funny it happened after all these years. Delayed reaction I suppose, no father should ever have to deal with what he dealt with, both of us were so ill in our own ways. A dog snuffled into the doorway of the boarded-up shop, its intention had been to urinate but seeing Alison it changed its mind and sniffed at her ankles, a tawny matted thing it was, tongue lolling pinkly in the heat, a man's voice shouted a name, a command, Hello said Alison, hello, but before she could bend down to bestow a proper greeting, dogs were so much simpler than people, the animal was gone. Unthinkingly she followed, the doorway had been grimy, posters peeling off the cheap boarding, it wasn't only dogs that urinated there, no place to be when you were filled up with a light so heavenly yet nothing like the light of the sun, how strange, how wonderful to have discovered it so late in life, well I'm only forty-three, plenty of time left, and all thanks to Colleen, she was the one who'd unlocked it. You can't think of God, God's unapproachable, but through Jesus Christ, Lord, Kyrios, you can find a way. Just those few words spoken and heard and a key turned, an electric bulb went on, how right she'd been, now Alison could meditate all day on Jesus, through and in Jesus she was able to understand this clear-flamed light that was love that even now returned her own love unconditionally, exponentially, right here in the street it was happening, grace, how beautiful were all the people around her. Was this what they called being

105

born again? Truly, the ways were mysterious by which she'd been brought here. Dust blew up from the gutter, the tiniest swirl, on the tarmac of the road where the cars trundled from one set of traffic lights to the next to the next a patch of oil shone out rainbow stripes, it felt like a reward seeing Colleen tonight though she knew she mustn't think of it that way, the girl's long absences from her life these days were a personal tragedy, yes that did sound a bit over the top but even so. Colleen's faith had never wavered, right from the start she'd been the real thing and sure this trip to the Holy Land would happen some day but to follow the girl, to join her in that life, the throb, the happiness, start again in purity, first a postulant, then a novitiate, final vows, it all begins with a knock on the cloister door said the literature, already she'd visited the place on a vocation retreat without Joe knowing, just a weekend, pretended she'd gone to her sister's—

Oh! Her phone! She'd switched the ringer off before going into the travel agent's. It was politer that way, so many conversations these days interrupted by buzzes and snatches of music. She dug the phone out from her bag, checked for messages, in the sunlight it was too bright to see the display, she went into a shop, that was better, ringer on, three messages in this short time, two voicemails, none from Joe, all from Amanda Margaret, Came home early, job not done, no Joe, not answering his phone, there's blood by the door, call me when u get this x. Neither when she dialled was Joe Forbes answering the phone to his own wife. Around and inside

Alison the clear-flamed light died away, how such a thing can be lost so quickly we can't say for sure, distraction is a powerful force, even the saints have been known to fall foul of it from time to time. When she hastened back out to the street the pavement was dirty and litter-strewn. Therefore, she was saying to herself, therefore, she repeated to herself, I take pleasure in infirmities, in persecutions, in distresses for Christ's sake – for when I am weak then am I strong.

11

IN the suburbs, the commuter conurbations, the satellite and dormitory towns, there you have space, you
have quiet, that's why people move there, the houses are
bigger, the only noise comes from the neighbour using
his lawnmower on a Sunday, naturally it's irritating but
he won't take long, he's considerate, you count him as a
friend. With his eyes closed Joseph listened to the sounds
of this world. He was sat at home on the porridgey sofa
in the front room or the lounge or the sitting room,
whatever you have been brought up to call it, his arms
arranged somewhat rigidly by his sides, knowing full
well that the messages would be piling up on his phone
and no wonder, what a position to have left Amanda
Margaret Hollander in, a job half done, no hot water or
central heating, not only unprofessional on his part but
a terrible abuse of the rights of householders to boot.
Since he'd turned off the handset some time ago however it was easier to continue avoiding it, to massage his
temples occasionally with the cleaner parts of his hands,
to keep his eyes shut, to examine in detail any noise

coming his way. In actuality the suburban air was not so tranquil, scaffolding clamps were being thrown into a bucket somewhere close by, boards were coming up, a train whined, a power tool thundered, it didn't matter where you were someone was always using a power tool. Nearer, inside the house, the Forbes's downstairs clock ticked, comforter, maybe, anti-annihilation device, maybe. Distantly a siren sounded.

Sirens. Even now he could call the police. No, immediately he dismissed the idea, no way of knowing how it might end. But he would have to tell Alison. How? Sit down, I have something to tell you. Something happened today. Prepare yourself for a shock, guess who I saw today. Here, I've made you a stiff drink, you'll need it (but Alison didn't drink) – there was no good way. Paths crossed, an encounter, unexpected collision of the vectoral. But she had a right to know, a right to defend herself, the poisoning when it happened all those years ago had not been nearly as amateurish as the defence barrister in his grand robes had suggested, carefully Edward had chosen to pour into Alison's drinks ethylene glycol which was sweeter and went unnoticed rather than embittered propylene glycol, oh yes there was a wide and comprehensive selection of antifreezes out there, a regular cornucopia of them in fact. The mannikin, the homemade altar, that was kids' stuff, a bit spooky perhaps but Edward was too intelligent to ever take it seriously, it had been a dark game he'd felt like playing for a while, whereas administering regular doses of ethylene glycol, that was something else altogether, that was of a different magnitude. Christ he'd been lucky to catch him that afternoon red-handed, if another two or three days had gone by... Unless Edward wanted to be caught? That had never occurred before. Another conundrum. Could it really be possible that everything he'd heard that afternoon, Diego, the parole board, the wealthy Arabs and Americans, was true? The Mahdi's knife with its three pineapple-top blades – you don't pick something like that up just anywhere. Nothing could look more jihadist. Tool of execution, but surely that wasn't the message. Did he leave it behind on purpose? Still there in the canvas bag inside the van.

Within the concavity made by his body in the sofa he shifted slightly, he adjusted his position, despite the urgency of these thoughts there seemed no compelling reason to stand up in the next five minutes, the next ten minutes. It struck him as unlikely that Edward would appear any time soon to play such a wild role. Paranoia has a lot to answer for and sometimes the wisest course of action is to wait. Besides he was washed out, drooped, the dial of futility beat higher. When next he opened his eyes he saw it was half past four and the room filled with afternoon light. He'd planned on being done and dusted by now or finishing up at least, loading his tools into the van, preparing to take Amanda Margaret's money, planning on taking anything else she might have to offer, how laughable, but he'd very much wanted to come back with that money and leave it on the kitchen table for Alison to see, dutiful husband, dutiful wife. Instead there was only failure, the half-finished cylinder job, the lacerated fingertips, the aura, Christ it had been bad, no wonder he felt so drained, a miracle he'd been able to get in the van and drive anywhere, adrenalin it must have been that kept him going. Well this was the other side of it, empty and full of blackness like maybe he'd fade away. Possibly the knife wasn't even worth much, possibly it was a junk-shop find. With superhuman effort Joseph rose from the sofa, in his mind an intention had formed to go to the kitchen sink, to remove the plasters and wash his hands, for the minute he'd come through the front door he'd flopped down so they were still unclean from the work undertaken earlier. Then a second intention, examine the fingers and thumbs. Was his skin really thinning as the doctor had said, how could it be? But the perpetualness of these rooms. A house too large for them ever since Edward had gone. The furniture he'd played on or around as a child, that was gone too, the scratches and bashes where he'd crashed his toy cars or fallen or tried to peel away the wallpaper were erased or repainted, Alison had insisted on that when she purged the house of his presence, the new suite arriving, the oatmeal-complexioned sofa and its companion chairs, those were her ways of dealing with it and who was he to question, it was not him who had been identified as a villainous imposter by their own grown child. Even the family photos, the portraits and holiday snapshots, had been on her list till he confronted her then stole them away and hid them in the garage under his plumbing supplies where she never looked. A room, a television, a little bookshelf, in the corner a Cross not overwhelming in size, was it so different from a prison cell? The Cross a gift from Colleen of course, damn her bony-faced French meekness. The consolation she'd given Alison was outrageous, once she'd wormed her way in, once she'd established herself, there was no way he'd been able to compete either from outside as Joseph her husband or from inside attempting to play her religious games, twice for example he'd gone along with her suggestion, Alison's suggestion, Let's try praying together, let's read the Bible together. Why not, try anything twice but what a waste of time it had been, total rubbish, galaxies and worlds created in six days and on the seventh God puts his feet up, how anyone could bring themselves to believe this stuff he had no idea. And then shortly afterwards the way her and Colleen were sudden bosom-buddies and pale-skinned and trembling with the black hair that Joseph had to admit he found enticing the girl had sat through *every day* of the trial like some modern-day Joan of Arc. A parasite, that's what she was, a parasite on other people's dramas and misfortunes. Well, she was out of the way now, well and truly out of the way, walled up, Get thee to a nunnery, you said it as a joke but Colleen had actually gone and done it. So let her remain there with the other tremblers. What did they do all day anyway, these Sisters of the Sacred Heart? On impulse as he passed the small bookshelf Joseph picked out Alison's Bible, he opened it, he looked at it, the lines that were marked, the pages that were turned down, others bookmarked with bright paper strips, were they colour-coded according to some system, who cared, he did – now don't go getting dirty fingerprints on it. All the same she'll be pleased to know I'm reading it. Paul, the Apostles, Revelation at the end,

Genesis at the beginning, words of command, words of guidance, words of healing, you could lose yourself in this all right, back and forth he turned the thin pages looking at the passages his wife had marked, the sayings of Jesus, the arrest of Jesus, Jesus as a stranger on the road to somewhere or other, then something caught his eye in Luke, Luke the favourite. There was a man who had the spirit of an unclean demon and he cried out with a loud voice, Let us alone! What have you to do with us, Jesus of Nazareth? Have you come to destroy us? And beside the printed word demon was written another word in black ink that said EDWARD. Further on, Then Jesus called the twelve together and gave them power and authority over all demons, and again in black ink EDWARD. Further on, While he was coming the demon dashed him to the ground in convulsions, and once again next to demon, EDWARD.

Joseph replaced the Bible and fell back onto the porridgey sofa. Yes, rooms like this he had spent his whole life in, suburban, safe, we're told they're safe, never had he been in mansions or townhouses, never had he known shacks or ghettoes or high-rises, yet now and in a trice he felt threatened, sinisterisms flapped close, his perception of his wife's understanding of their son during the years since imprisonment and household purge had not been so close to the mark after all, here was revelation, here was shock, call him soft but he'd always imagined inside her a process taking place of slow easing, slow blurring, that was how it had been for him or that was how he'd believed it to have been before the breakdown. Now from one revealed and repeated word it seemed that Alison had taken a different approach altogether, silently, internally, a line had been drawn, silently Edward had been identified as one infected with droplet of Satanic essence, perhaps some part of Satan himself, and recalling the boy glowering entombed in the plexiglas hutch of the defendant's box as the judge read out the sentence it was all too easy to imagine him that way, enrolled amongst the ranks of the damned. And though Alison always seemed to have an unshakeable faith in the goodness of people, right from her and Joseph's very first weeks together he'd seen how she brimmed with the milk of human kindness, who *doesn't* believe in that, it's common, don't we see it every day, don't we flatter ourselves, how good-hearted we are, how especially considerate, if only others could be more like us – yet fewer are those who while investing in Good do so equally in Evil, and fewer still those individuals who having encountered it in everyday life feel compelled to do battle with it. Was Alison amongst this handful? Slumped once more and massaging his temples Joseph saw the truth. It was not so much a matter of certain cryptic remarks of hers from the past slotting suddenly into place as a tide retreating to reveal the implacable shoreline of her authentic attitude. Further thoughts. He might be collapsed like any manual worker exhausted at the end of his day's labour but now his mind was picking up speed. First an inescapable irony. A synonym, another term for Capgras syndrome, was Delusional Misidentification, what a mouthful, let's stick with Capgras for the moment, anyhow delusionally due to a shortcircuit of the mind the son believed his mother to be an imposter, from that followed the idea that his real mother was elsewhere, where this elsewhere might be had never been specified but if he acted against the replacement the true mother might somehow be restored. That was the logic (and what boy doesn't want his real mother around) that after some internal frenzying-up had made Edward go out and buy the sweet-tasting ethylene glycol. Now from the juxtaposition of the repeated word demon and the handwritten upper-case EDWARD and from the mental shoreline thus revealed it seemed Alison had made a delusional misidentification of her own. No doubt Colleen had a hand in it or more than a hand – for sure, the girl had got to her at a vulnerable moment. But the tarot card had been before Colleen. One had led naturally on to the other. Talk about offences against common sense! People *were* who they said they were, more or less. Edward's mother was Alison, Edward's father was not Beelzebub.

Other implications. If Edward equalled demon and if today he, Joseph, had helped the boy, by talking to him, buying him food, giving him money, then Joseph was the demon's helper and as such must be cast out. But without Alison he could not survive, a terrible admission to make even in the privacy of one's own mind. But not to tell her – that wasn't at all the kind of betrayal he'd imagined at the start of the day. In an instant he foresaw the whole scene of the telling, how it would play out, what would happen, after the immediate shock it could only serve to drive her further into the arms of God or Jesus, what even was the difference, further anyway from him. And already he was a cuckold for there could be no misunderstanding their current domestic arrangements, every night his wife shared the bed with another man, just to clinch the deal this man had promised her the bonus of eternal life, a nice trick if you can get away with it, no wonder he went on pulling in the millions. Once in the house there'd been a living breathing boy, now a supernatural presence squatted the floorspace. But Alison's belief in Him and by extension His dark opposite must have been the only navigable way she'd found to deal with what had happened, after all the living breathing boy had turned out to be not so nice, the living breathing boy had nearly done for her. If she should discover the knife in the van! What happened said Alison, the door stood open, blankly he stared up at her. I rushed home from work, I've got all these calls from Amanda, are you all right, oh Joe I'm so pleased to see you here, I thought – I don't know what I thought...

Watch out Joseph, that's our advice, watch what you say and do, everyone knows the most intimate thoughts have a way of ending up expressed unmistakeably on the face, that's why people wear such enormous sunglasses nowadays.

12

SOMETHING'S been overlooked, we realise. The woman
Alison Forbes around whom our narrative hinges has yet
to be described. Back in the sunlit streets close to the
travel agent's would have been a good place to do it, all
we really know of her physical attributes are the delicate
forearm hairs which ruffled in the artificial breeze, let's
start from there, let's complete the picture, in colour they
were blonde, that's good, let's have more, given his gender
our narrator would naturally be expected to concentrate
on those aspects which might be found attractive by a
man, he could for example remark on the length and
quality of her hair, the colour of her eyes, the shape of
her lips, the size of her breasts, how she keeps the years
at bay, in order to heighten the dramatic contrast he
might compare her quietly but unfavourably with the old
friend Amanda Margaret Hollander whom her husband
of many years had been sexually fantasising about only
that morning. Above all let us not draw attention to
the fact that no equivalent description has so far been
awarded to the man Joseph himself, presumably because

our narrator, finding male bodies unattractive, has little to say about it other than the ways in which it malfunctions, clearly he's trying to elicit sympathy on the cheap.

Creaturely, many-pocketed, generous, never flagrant – so was the woman Alison Forbes. What happened? she asked again. Nothing, answered the man Joseph. Automatic response, false report, it wouldn't do, as his wife clasped him round the shoulder he added, I had a funny turn, I had to come home, I was not able to to finish the job. Oh Joe, everything will be OK, it was a mistake to go back this early, how did you leave things with Amanda, do you want me to talk to her? Joseph nodded, nobody mentions this thing named humiliation when you sign up for life, nobody deems it worthy of recording in the little red book where height, weight and circumference of head are measured and plotted. Holding up a grimy hand Joseph showed Alison the two plasters that were still hanging on, filthy and rolled at the edges with their grey threads dangling. The aura, the migraine, whatever you call it, that came too, I thought my head was going to explode, all I could see was the lightning bolt, remember when I drew it for you. Alison nodded, she remembered, recently her health had been good but memories of intensive care units, haemodialysis, spiked crystals streaming in her blood were never far away, she was naturally sympathetic, how awful the poor man looked sprawled there on the sofa. Has it gone now? Joseph nodded, Yes. I hope you didn't drive like that she said, genuinely concerned and prepared to give him a telling off if he'd done anything so reckless. Joseph shook his head, No, only slowly, to get home. Come on, let's get you over to the sink and clean your hands, these plasters need to come off, I'll get some paracetamol too. Like a mother bear with cub Alison manoeuvred him up, she led him into the kitchen and over the sink removed the plasters, Joseph's skin underneath had gone a little white and wrinkled. It isn't too bad, he said, already trying to excuse himself. No, I can see they'd hurt. As she washed and dried the hands with kitchen roll she thought of the villages of Galilee where Jesus had performed the acts of his ministry, she thought of Capernaum, before today only a name but there it had been in the travel brochure, a place you could actually visit, wouldn't it be something to really go. Go into the garden she told Joseph, ushering him out onto the patio, for like everyone in these islands she put great stock in the curative power of bathing oneself in the nuclear radiation of the sun. And when he was comfortably settled on the lounger whose head section she adjusted thoughtfully in order to make him feel less of an invalid she disappeared upstairs to gather medical supplies from the bathroom cabinet.

Gone five and the heat hadn't dropped by a degree. Where was the boy now, where would he be spending the night? In the house of this Diego? Silent and unthinking in the dark warm centre of himself Joseph's decision had been made. Easier to digest like this: by keeping her ignorant he was protecting her rather than himself. It wasn't true but in time it might become a consoling lie he could get away with. Here then was much shame, the shame of having to lie in order to keep her because coping alone felt impossible both emotionally and financially. And even Edward released from prison managed on his own! Never see him again was the most likely outcome. Above all don't *go looking* for him. Motherfucking arsewipe of a day. Not to mention the matter of the hot water cylinder left unfinished, you don't walk out on a customer like that and expect to go on working as a plumber. Probably that was Amanda Margaret now, for inside the house he could hear Alison talking, her voice indistinct but unmistakeably engaged in a phone conversation, slightly tetchy, No, of course not, Only one night, these words came through clearly enough, a laugh, they were discussing him and what was to be done, then silence, let the other person speak, that's the way to deal with those who feel hard done by, such a skill of listening Alison had, such a gift. Ten minutes later she reappeared in the little suburban garden with a tube of Savlon, some fresh plasters and a strip of paracetamol, these things she placed on a sunbleached and rainwashed plastic table which she dragged close to the lounger. Amanda's upset, actually she's distraught, she knew something had gone wrong, she said she thought you weren't quite right when she saw you this morning, you were acting a bit funny. Tell Amanda I'll be there first thing tomorrow, I won't charge her, except parts and they don't come to much. Oh Joe love, don't worry about Amanda, she's gone to spend a couple of nights with her boyfriend anyway, just till this is sorted out. Oh said Joseph, I didn't know she had a boyfriend. Gently Alison lifted her husband's hand and began to apply Savlon to the cuts, Don't put the new plasters on until this has had time to soak in.

How long's that been going on? How long's what been going on? This new boyfriend of hers. Oh, I don't know, a couple of months, you know what she's like. Alison smiled, Did I tell you the last time I saw her she told me she believes in reincarnation? No, you didn't. Oh yes, in a previous life Amanda was the wife of a pharaoh, no less!... now take these. From the strip Alison popped two chalky tablets, she fetched water, paracetamol might be the answer to most things but they couldn't be taken dry. Joseph placed them in his mouth and swigged the water and swallowed. You must have done some of it, you must have done a lot of it, otherwise your fingers wouldn't be in this state, did you wear the gloves? Yes, most of the time. You need to wear them all the time, as for the aura it was unlucky but they are becoming rarer, I make a note of when they happen, I jot it down in a little notebook. Do you? said Joseph in surprise, he had not been aware that his health was being monitored in this way. Yes, they're becoming less frequent, I'm confident they'll disappear soon. After this it seemed they had nothing more to say to each other though it wasn't necessarily a problem, here were a couple who often sat silent and easy in each other's company. Alison fetched a garden chair and unfolded it beside her husband, after a minute or two she reached across and squeezed the fingers of his undamaged right hand, once it would have been a simple squeeze of affection, this is just a hump in the road, it's nothing compared to what we've been through, we'll get through this together, now along with these vague and still present sentiments came an additional meaning, rarely did she say it out loud but Joseph knew very well what it was. I'll pray for you, I'll pray for you. And there – that was it, somehow the window gone finally, the chance sped past, irrecoverable moment, never could he now say, Look, there's something I need to tell you, or some variation of it, seven years ago her son and only child had been declared dead and thrust into oblivion, so strong she'd been then, so resilient since, the news would destroy her, by destroying her it would destroy him, never come back Edward, never come back, good riddance once and for all, say it over and over till you believe it. So you're OK out here on your own? Where are you going? Just upstairs for a while, Alison said, would you like me to get you something to eat? No, I'm not hungry. Crackers and cheese? No, really, I'm fine. Alison stood up, all day the sun had been high and unmoving, now the first mellowness of evening came borne in upon its rays, the first shadow-stubs pooled on the ground, but still no cloud, not one, another sticky night lay ahead. And then I've got my group, she added hesitantly, Monday night, remember? Oh yes, your group. I could… I could cancel if you like – if you wanted me here? No, no, you go. Are you sure? Joseph shrugged, he looked at her about to walk inside, some of the paving slabs he'd used to finish off the patio ages ago had settled out of line with the rest, when had that happened, he'd have to relay them, how irritating, Sure I'm sure. She smiled, she went in, he was alone.

Very quiet he lay on the lounger. His hairline oozed balls of sweat, the top of his head was damp too, so was his back, about him the walls of evening sunlight thickened and rose giving the impression, it was more than an impression, of being stuck at the bottom of a golden seamless well. What he was going to do next he hardly knew but so much was happening inside that reacting to exteriorities seemed unnecessary for the time being, a mass of thoughts, emotions and memories were on the move like parts of a cityscape churned by earthquakes, the heat roiling down on him cooked together all these constituent parts until presently out of the hot storm came simplification, two possibilities, he could either pay attention to the pressure that was building inside, the sinewy bag containing the secret that was threatening to blow already, or he could inflate the bag further, artificially pump it up, swamp the explosion when it came then surrender and prostrate himself before oceanic self-pity. Such thoughts, maybe it was the plumber in him accustomed to brooding in plasmic images. To think that when he'd first heard it he'd laughed out loud – What, Alison, an imposter! The room was hygienic and spacious, with charts on the walls, stickers on the sides of the computers, these stickers and charts spoke of processes and things that were easy to understand but when the talking started there was nothing like that, only more questions. No, Capgras isn't hereditary so there's no need to concern yourself with that, he didn't get it from you or your wife. No, we really don't think he's putting it on. One more question, I'm sorry, I know we've asked this before but it's what we neurologists have to do, did Edward ever suffer a bang or blow to the head? No said Joseph. Hang on, wait, wait a minute... yes, I think my wife did mention something once. The consultants glanced at each other. Is there anything more you can tell us about that, how old was he at the time? I don't know, five, six, I wasn't around much then, I was working a lot, working and sleeping, that's all I was doing. Joseph had nothing more to say on the subject because he knew nothing more. It's just that it's important we have as much information as possible, the younger consultant said, perhaps if Mrs Forbes would come in and talk to us? Joseph shrugged, unable to think of a polite way of saying, Not a chance in hell, she'll never agree. Yes, we do understand the details of the case are unpleasant but, you see Mr Forbes, the situation is rather complicated and to us it seems Edward may be as much a victim as your wife. Oh, that argument had played big in court. Oh, that one had been tussled over all right. And since that time the doctors had used Edward's case to lay claim to the word expert, they were consulted wherever this rare condition cropped up, perhaps from now on it would not be so rare, perhaps there were many in the wider population who had gone undiagnosed. Yes, those who'd kept themselves within socially acceptable limits! Inside Joseph the stress was increasing, the flesh-like rivets of the sinewy bag were straining, they were screaming, fibres popping one by one, these memories of the neurologists had served to push away the warm allure of self-pity, with sourness he wondered whether Alison upstairs in the box-room study was getting in some good value-added praying. Excessive, doing it now when she also had her group tonight but apparently you could never have enough of it, or of reading the Bible. It kept you before the mainsail of your own life she'd told him some time recently. Possibly at this very moment she was meditating upon the demonic but long-ago attempt to end her life and take possession, presumably, of her soul. And the group, this Monday night group where she had instruction or took part in discussions or whatever it was they did, he wasn't sure of the exact format except they celebrated Mass at the end, never miss an opportunity to celebrate Mass, why didn't someone just go ahead and make a breakfast cereal out of those damn wafers and have done with it, every morning you could load up on Eucharistic goodness, better than vitamin C, now there's a business opportunity, the group in any case was becoming too influential in her life, too important, why hadn't he seen it before. Not that he could prevent her from going – she'd even used it to wriggle away on the one occasion he'd asked her directly about this matter of a blow to the head, We'll talk later, she'd said, I can't stop now, I'm late for the group, but they never did talk later for it was after that particular night that the never mentioning Edward had begun. And thirty minutes on the internet, when he pursued a more medical line of inquiry, was enough to make anyone give up because from one search there'd come a hundred answers, from another a hundred more, mostly they disagreed with each other, they ranged from the moronic to the impossibly technical. Suddenly he leaped into the golden air, this pressure had to come out one way or another, the explosion, it was intolerable, he needed a blowout, a blowjob, yes that was it, a spiritual, emotional or psychological blowjob, maybe even a simple sexual one, where to get it from he had no idea, there'd been nothing like that with Alison for a long time. Well then, he'd put a shirt on and go out, there'd be plenty of people around on a warm night like this, he'd prowl about and see what was happening. Yes, that was what he wanted to do, he wanted to prowl about. At the very least achieve a state of inebriation before many more hours went by.

13

Extending his newly plastered fingers to the door-knob, Joseph found instead the entrance to the public house swinging open to receive him. Someone was on their way out, politely they held the door for him, Joseph murmured Thanks and went inside. The place was in gloom, two men only at the bar, one at one end, one at the other, both looked at him but neither spoke. Taking a stool equidistant from the two Joseph ordered a lager, the barman poured it and handed it over, he too a member of the wordless tribe. On the television a team in red had claimed a free kick against a team in yellow, this summer there were no international tournaments but they'd dredged up a game from somewhere, South America probably. If a spectacular goal should be scored Joseph might watch, otherwise it held no interest for him. Over his shoulder but now in the process of being hung from a brass hook beneath the lip of the bar was the canvas bag left behind by Edward, to Joseph's reappraising eye it had about it a dynamic or militaristic look, anything might be inside, state secrets, valuable trading information, if someone asked he would have the opportunity to give an enigmatic reply. But nobody did ask, no brilliant but jaded personalities stood eager to engage Joseph or soothe him in his moment of despondency, here was no hub of freewheeling confidence, the pub was simply a hostelry in a minor English town, parts of it barely literate, its citizens dedicated to the national pastime of defending their parking spaces from neighbours or random interlopers. Neither were there any dirt-of-the-earth lumpenproletarian types happy to perform poignant or hilarious monologues. What a disappointment this place is, in short it's deader than dead. Meanwhile wrapped and snug inside the canvas bag lay the Mahdi's knife, not only was it better away from the house but the man Joseph had an idea that later on, somewhere private and alone, he would like to take it out and look at it and think. Despite everything Edward was still his son, he had seen all the milestones, the first smile, the first lock of hair, the first word, he'd caught the boy when he began to walk, instructed him in the knack of the bicycle, how to kick a football with the side of the foot in order to attain more accuracy, sentimental these things might be but they lived and in living proved they did not mean nothing. Aren't you going to drink that? said the man nearest the television set. Joseph glanced up from the immersion of his thoughts and saw the man looking at him and at the pint of ice-cold lager which his hand without conscious instruction had lifted and pressed to his perspiring face. A good feeling this, he liked it, back and forth he rolled the glass over his forehead, he closed his eyes and reopened them, he watched the studs of moisture ooze down the skin of the glass, the way their tails crossed and joined, never underestimate the power of water, this he knew because like any plumber he had both created floods and dealt with them. I plan to said Joseph, lowering the glass and taking from it a long drink. But after a few more sips with each becoming less heavenly he got to wondering why he had ordered this in the first place, he didn't even like lager, too gaseous, it swelled in his stomach. It was just that lager in summer was the rule, what a strange mixture of notions and ways in which to behave our friend Joseph has picked up, no consistency at all, no doubt he'd admit as much if we asked him directly. Anyway the pint would have to be taken slowly or he'd end up bloated like a tropical tree frog. Now where had that come from, many were the files stored in his personal image-lexicon but amphibians did not feature prominently among them. Then glancing at the door-end of the bar he realised that the other man had been trying to catch his eye and supplementing his efforts with a peculiar opening and closing of the mouth, a word about to be spoken cancelled and invalidated on the cusp of escape. Immediately the man saw Joseph looking at him he turned his face away but a minute or so later he was at it again, attempting to catch Joseph's eye, opening his mouth to speak, perhaps he had an entertaining story to tell, some witty anecdote about this place whose atmosphere was hardly uplifting and not at all what Joseph was after – then came the scratching out of the impulse and the trying to hide it behind a hearty lifting of a glass to his lips. Overall he gave the impression of a gulping regretful fish. Maybe he has something wrong with him, Joseph thought, something in his head, in his brain, some abnormality, yes, a hundred years ago he'd be the village idiot and nothing more need be said, these days his condition would be precisely defined some-where, it's even possible that modern treatments have improved his functioning to the extent that he's able to sit at the bar of a public house like any ordinary lonely male customer.

Joseph pushed his lager away and shouldered the canvas bag. This was no good, he wanted to be somewhere where at least he could look at women. The gulping man evinced surprise that a half-full pint should be abandoned, that too was against the rules, Joseph retrod the gloom, out-side some high clouds were drifting in at last, later the light might fade to green, these green skies of summer were his favourites in all of the year. Since the public house was on the periphery of town he now undertook to walk to the centre, there it would busier, something might pull him in, something might happen. Past the leisure centre he went, even on a night like this there would be good competitors inside playing badminton, playing squash, circuit training. What courses might his life have taken if he'd been born rich, highly intelligent, overpoweringly handsome, a thousand years into the future, a thousand years into the past? Inside him the memory of the encounter with Edward was shifting, morphing to occupy more of those darker zones which he now realised had been more or less peaceable until the boy's appearance that afternoon. At the start when

Edward had gone away it'd been like this, just like this, the guilt, the regret, ideas of self-destruction, God the way he'd burned up that mannikin, the rage, how long had he laboured to persuade himself of the falsity of his feelings, months, years, trying to convince himself they were dealt with, finished and over, that everything was all right but it wasn't, of course it wasn't, it never had been and that's what caused the breakdown. For a long time he knew in his secret self it was coming, for a long time he held it off because of Alison, then he couldn't any more, and now just when the tunnels and galleries had begun to seal, what terrible places they'd been, waystations of loneliness and despair, here they were gaping afresh, scaled to a different size in fact each was like a pore in a universe-sized skin of sadness. I'll pay you back, Edward had told him. I'll pay you back. How was he going to do that, when, had he meant it or was it just one of those things people said? At the next junction Joseph saw too late a dog turd and stepped partially into it but the excrement was so desiccated it didn't matter, he stomped the workboot he was still wearing against a nearby wall, another ten steps and it would be gone. Up ahead the pavements were becoming livelier, the square, sounds reached him, music, conversation, laughter, this was more like it. Here came the statue of the one famous man the town had produced. In reality this famous man had been born in the next settlement along and the two still argued over him, China in any case was where two centuries ago this man had spent most of his life, China was where he'd accumulated the fortune which surely he was entitled to.

This would do. This place Joseph had not been inside before. The Rampant Hedgehog it was called. He paused to look up at the sign over the door, stylish and striking, a giant hedgehog reared in front of a hastily braking car, the posture of the animal suggesting simultaneously that not only was it ready to do battle with the car, in revenge and perhaps memoria of its brethren flattened on highways up and down the land, but that in addition it was becoming aroused, that it considered the car a potential mate, its eyes glinted with unmistakeable intent, cleverly the maker of the sign had concealed behind the bonnet of the car a presumably engorged hedgehog's penis. Summertime, heatwave time – beneath the sign, sitting at tables or standing around upended barrels that served as tables young people were gathered, the men were tall, the girls pretty, no-one wore too much of anything, here and there older groups mingled, maybe Joseph would bump into Amanda Margaret Hollander and her new boyfriend here, wouldn't that top things off nicely. But fortunate that it was Monday night for on Fridays and Saturdays he believed they had bouncers on the door who would demand a peek inside the military-looking canvas bag and imagine the uproar if the triple-bladed Sudanese knife were discovered. Still he'd die a heroic death grappling against their choke-holds and in the final moment of his final moments might even shout out Allahu Akbar, God is Great, with such a sentiment Alison could hardly disagree and it would get everyone else's backs up for sure. As he entered the Rampant Hedgehog and ordered a whisky, No he said to the barman, he didn't care how many types they had, the first one that came to hand or the most popular, Laphroaig, said the barman and Joseph nodded, But make it a double, make it a double, as he took his first mouthful a girl came and stood beside him, because of the layout of the bar and the arrangement of the other people waiting or being served she stood close, she was wearing a white halter-neck top and the bare skin of her upper arm brushed the bare skin of his elbow, he had the sleeves of his shirt rolled partway up, it was a way to look younger than he really was. Sorry, he said, Sorry, she said, well that was it, the conversational opener, he was permitted now to speak to her while she waited dangling from the tips of her fingers a plastic payment card. He could talk to her about the weather, not that interesting a subject but something at least, he could offer to buy her a drink, if he did it casually and with a carefree-enough smile, roguish, take-it-or-leave-it, she might accept but this kind of smile he'd never been able to conjure at the best of times and certainly not tonight. Did you get your fingers trapped in something? asked the girl. What? said Joseph. Your fingers, what happened to your fingers? Oh, I cut them, that's all. The girl shrugged, that was the end of her interest, as she leaned forward to glide the card over the payment terminal her perfume flew up his nostrils, so feminine and unlike anything Alison would ever use it sent yellow sparks across the field of his brain. Taking a deep drink of whisky he sought to magnify the effect, it worked, it was dizzying, reckless escape, the bare back revealed by the halter-neck top was turned completely towards him now, all at once he wanted to press her to him, the greasy pyramidal hair, the skinny shoulders, bury her in an embrace, then by some magical trick that this ultimate embracing would facilitate he'd be able to transfer to her a portion of his woes, a trouble shared is a trouble halved or so they say. Still he might speak to her, still there was time but always this meekness getting in the way, what to say, what, how about this, My wife thinks my grown-up son is a demon, it sounded like the start of a joke, stick around for the punchline, then she'd see and recognise the heart-rending look in his eyes. Let's go over there, that quiet corner, no-one'll bother us, everyone's outside enjoying the last of the sun, no the difference in age doesn't matter to me, tell it your own way, take your time, only say what you feel ready to say, what sympathy she'd have. Instead she was leaving, bearing drinks away into the soft evening light, it was painful to watch her go, actually painful, someone like that would never give him a second look, no nor a first one either, nothing to do therefore but gird and turn stony-hard inside, nothing to do but throw the whisky down your throat. One day she'd be as old and haggard as he was and then no-one would want to touch her, he'd be gone and she'd be gone too, both of them and everyone else here atomised in the fires of sun and time, it was a consoling thought, he felt gladdened, girl'd looked like a weird pelican anyway, lopsided from the wind.

A note of bitterness has entered our narrative, it wasn't wanted yet let's not assume that the reality of things rested in perfect counterpoise to the man Joseph's unique and gloomy mood. In truth the Rampant Hedgehog was less than half full, the bar staff were weary, the laughter at most of the outside tables was weak, at others the conversation strained or non-existent, hardly a hive of jollity then, was it possible that the heat of the sun which for days had attacked the moisture in the earth was doing the same to the brain fluids of the bar's customers? No snap to the proceedings as Joseph detected going outside himself, it must be the whisky vision bringing on this necessary correction, Same again, he'd told the barman, same again. He stood beside a vacant barrel-table, he drank and watched the girl and her boyfriend, their interaction, there was nothing he, Joseph, possessed that she wanted, there was nothing he had to tell her or any of them here except the story of his life which was insignificant, but at least the whisky was travelling well, from the centre of his body to the circumference it had slipped, pleasurably it chafed his capillaries, it pacified the numberless prickles of his skin-nerves. Enough of this stuff and you could melt the tundra of yourself and the tundra of those around you, take an axe to it, yes, and then when you sent out those authentic waves of friendship and warmth you would know they'd been received, that they'd been recognised, in return would come universal love and you'd end up, who knows, as some wise old man, green, generous and fertile still. But always it was just out of reach, this transformation, this melting, notoriously the daydreams of the weak and voiceless tend towards the realm of fantastical power, as an aside we would like to know whether the fantasy life of those commanding genuinely tyrannical infrastructures ever include rhapsodies on the theme of poverty and bad

135

housing, possibly they do, there's nothing more perverse than human nature.

Joseph upended the glass and shot the remainder of the whisky down his oesophagus. Some doors away stood a late-night convenience store, he'd go in there and stock up, the time was approaching to remove himself to a more private place and take out the Mahdi's knife and see if he couldn't wrestle from it some meaning that he might have missed earlier. After all he hadn't unwrapped the thing entirely from its rags, buried in those folds there could be a card, Diego's business card, a scrap of paper, a phone number – anything. He hurried past the statue of the man who had done things in China and entered the convenience store. Behind the counter the proprietor stood to attention, he'd been dozing, in this weather who could blame him. In a trice he was fully awake and eager to serve, eager to please, that's how the people of this town liked those few souls who'd blown in from the vastness of Asia. Joseph nodded, the proprietor nodded, upstairs his kids were doing their homework, around the square a percentage of the local demographic was getting drunk, later there'd be shouting, at the weekends it was worse, forget Stratford-upon-Avon, any tourist visiting these islands should come here if they want to see the oaken heart of England. Across the lately mopped floor Joseph padded, it was the usual sort of place, food for those in a hurry, harassed mothers, enervated pensioners, packs of schoolkids, then the wall of alcohol which was what really kept business moving. In front of the big bottles of whisky Joseph's hand hovered. They were all much of a muchness, the only thing anyone cared about was the price and he was the same, he lifted one out, the label showed a grouse or some other Scottish-looking bird, it would fit nicely inside the canvas bag, what need was there to go about looking like an alcoholic. Then glancing along the magazine rack he saw something that caused him to stop. A magazine, a very particular magazine on the top shelf, he took it down and turned the pages, they were glossy, the pictures fascinating, alluring, what a find, no reason he shouldn't take this too. Together he put magazine and whisky on the counter, the proprietor scanned the items and spoke an amount, and as Joseph handed the money over he thought with not much in the way of advance contrition that if he drank this whole bottle tonight or even most of it then finishing Amanda Margaret's hot water cylinder would in all likelihood not happen tomorrow. Oh well, the new boyfriend'll keep her warm, she can wash at his place, tomorrow I'll feel bad about it, tonight I won't, the blowout still needs to come, that's most important, that's the priority.

On a grey-brown open palm Joseph's change came back to him. There on the counter too, chained to the cash register and almost lost among a clutter of paperwork was a plastic collection tin, yellow and stickered with wounded technicolour children. At the top of the sticker was a red crescent, God knows where the money really goes, some mosque somewhere. And from there? But as the proprietor placed the change in Joseph's hand he smiled an encouraging smile, whether this was for himself or his customer we can't say for sure but the cheeks covered with scars of childhood acne certainly puckered into a manifestation of friendliness. Where does the money go? Joseph said, tapping the collection tin, some nerve it took to ask the question directly. The children, the children, answered the proprietor. Joseph dropped his coins into the slot, maybe it actually did, as he exited the convenience store he found himself considering what it would be like to be a Muslim, praying all those times a day to that black cube in Mecca, was somebody buried inside it, a rug, a bow, a kneel, forehead to the floor, seven times a day was it, what a commitment, then once in your life you had to make the pilgrimage to the black cube itself, you had to circle it or touch it, every year you heard of people stampeded to death. Plus there was the fasting and the not drinking, well that was too much, you had to draw the line somewhere.

14

Soon he reached the outskirts of town, where had the miles gone, nowhere, the place wasn't that big. Here we find our friend Joseph altered once more, how his moods change, they're like the proverbial shifting sands, where's the good guiding twine of common sense that each of us plucks at from the moment we leave the amniotic pool, it looks as if it's been loosened catastrophically, witness the way he's staggering this way and that, almost into the road itself. The knife and its wrappings have been searched, nothing found, mouthfuls of whisky have been sucked down, the magazine purchased in haste is forgotten, perhaps that'll change if Joseph stops drinking, but anyway he won't stop walking now. What's there to go back for? An empty house or a house occupied by someone to whom he's becoming a figure of marginal interest. However much Alison might protest otherwise, Joseph knows the truth. Besides, look at these skies. They're something. Real cloud kingdoms of infinite type, streets and staircases picked out in orange and pink, cloud harbours, cloud ships, so slowly they move, why not keep going towards them. The jet stream's up there too, somewhere, trying to wake up. No loyal friend appeared to take Joseph by the shoulders and shake some sense into him, no brisk voice ordered him return to home fires, unexpectedly we discover ourselves recalling here one of the most memorable scenes in all of English literature, an animal named Mole whose heart has been set aflame by the whisperings of a foreign voice is intercepted and turned back on his newly adventurous heels by a fellow creature named Rat, No need to go poking about abroad old chap, stay at home, it's all here, the world comes to us. Long have we prayed that no weasel playing truant from its frozen and inadequate tree-root shelter goes leaving a hole in the bottom of Mr Rat's boat one fine spring morning. Joseph in other words was walking rather than going for a walk, the two are different, one implies no retracing of footsteps. Moreover he'd only ever driven this way before and now looking down saw to his surprise that the pavement had disappeared and in its place was grass verge, withered and dusty from heat and the chemical outpourings of motor vehicles it might be but to his mind it was pleasant, always slab or concrete underfoot. Up ahead he believed there to be a proper sort of countryside though at this end of town he couldn't be sure. All the same he liked this staggering around like a tramp, it gave him a thrill, so what if it was adolescent, the looks he was getting from the drivers of the cars that went by, the outrage, the indignation, it had been a long day for them and now here was some drunken idiot swaying into the road, what a loser, somebody better call the police, it's only a matter of time till he causes an accident. Ostentatiously Joseph swung the bottle of whisky, the brown grouse on the label blurred, the edges of many visible things had acquired a profound glow from the dying summer evening, the canvas bag that slapped his side was exciting too, in the most recent turns of logic taken by his mind which was now supple and now jingly he knew he would never see Edward again, that was over, that was over, the psychological hit would come later when he'd sobered up but what a gift the boy had left, this knife, how magnificent, how menacing, imagine bursting into Alison's study group waving it around, real Old Testament stuff, yes the first thing he'd do tomorrow would be set about reclaiming his wife from those bastard Bible bashers, he could see now he'd been too timid, too timid about everything.

The problem was these second thoughts, third thoughts, fourth thoughts that foamed around every subject his brain considered, they were no good because each brought in their wake their own second, third and fourth thoughts until before you knew it you were swamped, confused, totally lost. Cars flashed out of the sun like golden chariots, glances of people within, each car dumped upon him its parcel of hotness, the verge became thick and overgrown until he was having to labour through it, this was jungle, why didn't the council take it in hand. From a clump of arrow grass he snatched handfuls of darts and pelted the cars, close by a horn sounded, a driver thrust out a middle finger. Beneath Joseph's feet the ground was rising, becoming an embankment which meant he'd soon be on the bypass. That explained the increased traffic and its speed. Grasping at tufts with his free hand and feeling the canvas bag swing low by his knees he sought to ascend to the top, here were tall grasses flopped from the heat, thistles, tiny pink flowers, tiny blue flowers, they were beautiful, he stared at them, he wanted to remember them, briefly he saw over the crest of the embankment a straggled hedgerow and a dirt track on the other side leading away to farmland or something, who knows how the real countryside works, then his foot snagged in a hole, balance gone, tumble tumble and he was down at the bottom again. What a ride but he'd lost nothing, the whisky had rolled safely down too, lucky the cap was screwed on properly.

You nearly made me crash said a voice. A little way down the road a car had pulled in and a man was getting out, already the traffic had backed up, those who wanted to continue their journey would have to navigate this new obstacle, they would have to cross the white line and drive partially on the other side. Again the man spoke, he was striding towards Joseph, other drivers watched from other windows. Joseph stood up, he was too busy straightening himself out to care much, too busy untwisting and reslinging the canvas bag, it did look good, jaunty, the man or rather his shoulders and head entered his field of vision. What do you think you're doing? Joseph shrugged, how to respond, he'd fallen down a grassy bank, that much should be obvious to anyone. My girlfriend's in there said the man, jerking his thumb back at the car that had pulled in. What, Joseph said, can't she take care of herself, he failed entirely to understand what the presence or otherwise of this man's girlfriend had to do with anything. Don't insult a lady replied the man, come on, you're coming with me. What? Into the car, I'm taking you to the police, I've had it with your sort. What sort, what are you talking about? The man was large, his limbs were thick, the red maple leaf T-shirt he wore commanded people to visit Vancouver, a pizza-sized hand grabbed Joseph by the throat. Get off me, get off, he slapped at the man's pizza-sized hand till somehow it dislodged then tried to walk off along the verge but the man was coming after him, he caught Joseph's arm and shoved it up behind his back and tried to get him down on the ground, Joseph scrambled away just in time, he broke into a run, he was sobering up fast. Don't let him escape Robbie, cried a woman's voice. Call the police, shouted the man, he's resisting. In the road the traffic was moving once more, those drivers who'd been stuck had found some means of negotiating the obstacle, how ingenious are the ways of travellers, we're glad they'll get home on time. But the man was not giving up his pursuit of Joseph, possibly he remembered the famous Canadian motto, a Mountie always gets his man. Both of them were now struggling up the knotted grass of the embankment, Joseph slightly higher, nothing else for it, he turned and pulled out the Mahdi's knife, the crocodile-skin handle, the three pineapple-top blades. Once carried in the siege of Khartoum, here it was being used against an Englishman again, seeing it the man's eyes widened, he took a step back, to right and left Joseph swiped the murderous implement, this was a power trip all right, it gave him the audacity to bear down on the retreating man and retrieve the bottle of whisky from the place where it had landed. He's got a knife, screamed the man in disbelief. Lynsi, are you filming this, are you getting this? What? shouted the woman sat in the car. I said, He's got a knife, look at it, are you filming this on your phone? Oh Robbie, I told you, the battery's gone...

Steadily Joseph backed up the bank. It was easier to do now that he needed to do it and this time he didn't stop to look at the pink or blue flowers. At the top he checked with a glance to see where was the best place to break through the straggly hedge and onto the dirt track, he stuffed bottle and knife into the canvas bag, clutched the bag to his chest then ran, as he thought, like the wind.

15

Wʜᴇɴ the man Joseph knew nobody was coming after him he slowed to a walk, soon afterwards feeling safe and miles away he stopped. Here were tracks and paths only and the sound of traffic was little more than a drone. He dropped the bag and braced hands against knees, wobbly fire filled both legs, sweat sluiced his clothing, he needed to sit down, where, anywhere. The sun had gone, its light sweeping into other parts of the world, but at least the clouds still looked nice lit from below and they'd be like that for a while longer. Beside a rut he dropped, the pathside turf dusty and brittle, agricultural machinery must pass this way and that's why the ground was so gouged. Thirst. If anywhere nearby there'd been a puddle he would have slurped from that and though the thought of spirits now turned his stomach he shortly found himself putting the neck of the hot whisky bottle to his lips. Do it fast and don't think about it. Throwing back his head he then looked by accident straight into the sun, no it hadn't all gone, one last molten lozenge floated there above the distant treeline, whisky burn, retina burn, stupid, stupid, he snapped his eyes shut but a fiery image throbbed in the dark, dear God not the aura again or anything like it, I've had enough visual disturbances for one day. But Alison said she was monitoring them, she said they were going away.

After some minutes of head-hanging he remembered the third item inside the canvas bag that his son had bequeathed him. Firewater, a weapon, now a tome of printed and probably dubious material, truly the man Joseph is equipped for a quest, let's hope that our ending is cooked up and ready for deployment, nobody likes to be disappointed. He took out and opened the magazine, back in the convenience store it had caught his eye not just because he and it shared a name but because someone had spoken to him about it earlier in the day, on its pages the women were fully clothed, so were the men, they were billionaires with ramparts of gold behind which the reader was cordially invited. In the dusklight he read the story of Kimberley, she was young, she was charming, a God-fearing Christian, they're everywhere when you start looking, she'd begun by chopping lettuce for burger buns, nowadays she owned the burger chain itself, investors wanted to invest, they wanted a slice of the action but she swore she'd never sell, no IPO would be forthcoming, it would always be a family affair. She was hot property, worth a couple of billion already. Joseph turned the pages, more and more stories of success, mostly these others were of young men who'd made fortunes by inventing apps for smartphones. He took another glug of whisky, that one was more palatable, he searched the magazine for other pictures of Kimberley, how could he meet her, how could he get to know her, somehow he'd have to join the billionaires' club too, find something to exploit. Into the rut he stared, it was cracked and hardened by the heat, in the diminishing light it struck him suddenly as statuesque, here was the curl of a breaking mudwave, there a glazed trough, here a parapet, there a turret, the whole patterned with intricate and well-regulated platelets, a world of detail you could get lost in, why not, neither was the mud uniform in colour, it shimmered from silky white to steel blue, impossible to point to the place where these colours changed.

Experimentally Joseph poured two capfuls of whisky into the rut, he drank a third, he wanted to see how this rock-like mud reacted to an influx of liquid. If in this place he built a bender, it would be easy enough to find the materials, sticks and a tarpaulin were all you'd need, then he could study this rut all year round, people did that, they studied peculiar things over periods of time, months or years, they presented their findings in some artistic way and became famous. Getting down on his knees to look closer into the rut he felt with certainty that he could convince large sections of the public of its beauty, then he would be Lord of the Rut and need never fit another hot water cylinder or condensing boiler again. Perhaps like the young computer scientists he could create some app about it and that would carry him into the pages of Forbes magazine. Facerut, Rutface, Rutbnb, Instarut. Strange how the whisky sat there in a pool, the earth was too hard to absorb it, he smudged the pool about with an unplastered finger, stood up, the rut was tedious after all, monolithic, unresponsive, he felt himself yawn, twice in open court the defence barrister at Edward's trial had yawned, the judge had shot the man a quizzical look the second time, upon both of them in their grand robes Joseph wished disappointment and doom. Abruptly a motorbike crashed past, the heat of its engine, the rider wearing an open-faced helmet turning to grin or leer at Joseph. Eye-to-eye contact then gone, disappeared round a bend up ahead. Must've taken a bit of skill to buck the rut like that though. Inexplicably ghostly despite the engine roar. Ghosts, Christs, demons, devils – mad to believe in such stuff but in an isolated place like this with the light going it was easy to spook yourself. No wonder people went crazy for witch trials once.

Joseph followed the bike because that direction was as good as any other. He discovered a road, it might have been a private road but there were no signs saying so. Cut into the undergrowth on the far side was a space for turning, also a shipping container, Maersk it said on the side. He crossed the road with the trio of items stowed in the canvas bag and shimmied past the container, this was curious, with trees and a small hill rising the arrangement combined to form an obstacle, the intention evidently to prevent four-wheeled vehicles accessing the site beyond. Out of nowhere a disused quarry. In monochrome light Joseph entered it. He'd landed on the moon, Sea of Tranquillity, not so tranquil with the motorbike buzzing about however – seeing straightaway the rudimentary racetrack that had been laid out here. Sparrows fled as he climbed a spoil heap from where he could sit and watch, so often this activity of watching seemed the only thing left for a man to do these days. Two boys circled the track, one the now-helmetless rider of the motorbike, more properly a dirtbike since the engine and its housing were stripped to the bare minimum, dinosauric this machine looked in its roaring essentials, the other who was younger going round and round on a pushbike, a race between the two therefore an impossibility although various sectors of the track provided compensating interest, humps, hairpin bends, old quarry workings to avoid, what a place this was for thrills. But Joseph must have caught their attention for already the younger boy was flagging down the older and pointing, a halogen light was being shone directly at his eyes and the two were approaching on foot. Deciding he might need something to use as a bribe or payoff Joseph took out the whisky, miracle of miracles there was still a third left, he dangled the bottle between his hands, the boys were like things about to become shadows, they stopped at the foot of the spoil heap, they hesitated to climb it, they did climb it, again the halogen was shone in his eyes, it blinded, that was impolite. I'm lost, he said before either of the boys had a chance to say anything, how do I get back to town? Nice bag said the older boy, give it to me and I'll tell you. I don't want to, Joseph replied. The older boy shrugged, give it to me, I want to try it on, I want to see if it suits me. No. Why not? If I give it to you I won't get it back. Fucking state of you, you weren't here last weekend were you, let me try on that bag. I'll show you what's *in* the bag, if you tell me how to get back to town. In the failing light it was difficult to guess their ages. One eighteen perhaps, the other fourteen, or twelve, they might be brothers, they might hardly know each other. It's something to see, it belongs in a museum really, unexpectedly Joseph was discovering within himself a desire to impress, where had that come from, he hadn't been around boys this age for years. He put the bottle to his lips, this time the burn was negligible then he offered it up. No way am I drinking out of that said the older boy, think of the backwash. No backwash, Joseph answered, shaking the bottle at the younger boy who said nothing but took it and drank defiantly from it. You want to show us something? said the older boy, I bet you do, I bet you want us to touch it too, you fucking nonce. Again the halogen flashed in Joseph's eyes, this time it was his turn to shrug, by continuing to sit he retained a slight advantage over them, it made him vulnerable, a threshold they might not be prepared to cross. Standing up would be an invitation to violence, that was the unwritten rule of this encounter. But this need in parallel to impress or to make an impression. Nothing like that said Joseph, it's nothing like that, he unslung the canvas bag, the moment it was off his shoulder the older boy snatched it away, Joseph tried to stand but the older boy pushed him down and caused him to topple to one side, both boys meanwhile had retreated down the spoil heap, the older showing no intention of sharing anything with the younger. He was the owner now of Edward's canvas bag, he trotted for the dirtbike, picked up the machine and kicked the engine into life, the younger boy threw a stone at him then ran behind a bush, across the mud and gravel of the quarry floor the dirtbike sped away.

Never did you hear anyone talking of these green skies of summer even though they were quite regular – into the boundary layers of atmosphere up above the colour had filtered or assembled. There was no reason to stand up that the man Joseph could see, he might sleep here and go home tomorrow, the night was sure to be warm enough. Alison would have finished her Monday night group by now, she'd be back home and worrying about him, about his not being there, he knew he should call but what chance was there of a signal out here, none, almost none, at least he should check his phone, at least he should do that, then in what remained of the light he saw that the younger boy was creeping near, still grasping the whisky bottle. Joseph watched him drink from it, there couldn't be much left now, closer came the boy and when he was near enough for conversation, What was in the bag? he asked, he wouldn't let me see. Oh nothing, just some stupid magazine. There wasn't anything valuable in there? No, nothing. The boy smiled, You mean you were bullshitting him? Yes, bullshitting him, that's what I mean, that's exactly what I mean, the bag was cheap too, now throw me that bottle. The boy did so, Joseph caught it, he unscrewed the cap and tipped what was left of the whisky into the dirt of the spoil heap, I'm sick of this stuff, he announced. The boy came closer, he crouched down, Joseph looked at him silhouetted against the green sky, snubby nose, curly hair, the first stars were coming out, the boy was slurring slightly because of the whisky, what a vile and disgusting person he, Joseph, was, what had he been thinking handing it over like that, he wanted to reach out and hold this boy, he wanted to make some connection happen, how impossible, impossibility enough to make you cry. What happened here last weekend he said, not wanting the boy to go, not wanting to be alone, any question would do to keep him there. From a pocket the boy dug out a phone, he tapped and stroked the screen, by its light his face was illuminated, greeting-card image of innocence lit by Christmas candlelight or was that a memory from Edward's childhood, once he'd sung in church, the boy handed him the phone, the two of them were close enough for such an exchange to happen, it was a video, the boy wanted Joseph to watch it, well that was easy, a tap of the screen and it began, confusing at first to make out what was going on but the soundtrack was men shouting bellicose encouragement. Night-time, everything badly lit and the camera shaking about, shapes piling into each other – dogs they were, snarling and barking and running back and forth. Dogfight, crazy dogfight. No, there was something else, something tethered or chained to some part of the old quarry workings. The video blurred and ended. Did you see the vet? asked the boy. The vet? He was the one wearing the apron, he was the one that got it. Got what? From some dodgy zoo – the bear. What? Watch it again. Joseph did so, he hit the repeat button, yes, this time he saw a man in an apron, the man turned away when he saw he was being filmed, the dogs snarled and bit, the camera zoomed in, something fought the dogs but it could only go so far before the line yanked it back, dark and grainy, really impossible to tell. When Joseph returned the phone the boy's face was in darkness but by starlight and the vestiges of atmospheric green he saw two eyes glint liquidly, the boy was weeping, the whisky had gone straight to his head, again Joseph cursed himself, what could he do to make things right. It was only a baby bear said the boy unsteadily, it didn't know what was happening to it, all it knew was it was afraid. Joseph sat silent, he pretended not to see how the boy twisted his wrist in order to regain control. I didn't like it anyway. Neither did I, Joseph said. The boy got up and ran down the spoil heap, he needed to collect his pushbike, where was he going, to whom was he returning, Godspeed called Joseph. Godspeed he whispered when the boy had gone.

16

JOSEPH'S story is almost at an end, let us finish it briskly and without adornment. To reach him, however, we must needs first go through the woman Alison. Here she is, sitting at the small desk in the box-room of the family house, the tiny place she likes to call her study. In the past couple of years it's been her sanctum sanctorum but now she's considering a relocation. Upon the desk-top sit two books and a free-standing wooden Crucifix, a Cross, it might be better if this Cross had a base of some sort, then it wouldn't fall over so often, yet in truth she doesn't mind since every time it does it gives her an opportunity to pick it up and gaze at it. Something inside Alison is transforming itself into a true student of Christology. But what a night – quite different from usual! Father Howard had been there of course, beginning to end, setting out the chairs, fussing with his cuffs, tweaking his collar, how he did go on. No, she didn't need a point repeated three times before she was able to grasp it. And then the room had filled up, as much as it ever did, and the speaker came in apologising for being late, the trains, so unreliable but never mind, here she was, no, she only needed a glass of water and a minute to gather herself, then they could begin. How wonderful Colleen had looked! And the smile she'd beamed in Alison's direction! Not that she was *just* Colleen any more, eager-to-please Colleen from Clermont-Ferrand with its smokestacks and tyre-making plants. Behind her lay the period of discernment, the postulancy, the novitiate, now she was Sister Colleen, RSCJ, teaching, leading retreats, taking on new responsibilities. How well it suited her, so full of light it seemed, her skin so clear (no habit of course, the Society had given those up years ago), such purpose as she spoke about their work, their daily life with each other, their routine, the commitment to prayer, what prayer meant to her, such gravity she possessed, or gravitas, whichever it was, a seriousness but not of the overbearing sort, she'd grown up, that was it, or part of it. Anyway what presence she had nowadays, this girl who might have been Alison's daughter, the one she'd never had. Somehow just watching her you could sense the inner freedom and how much of it there was, beside her Father Howard looked dried up and dusty, far too anxious for the spirit to ever move inwardly, perhaps it never had done, not properly. And the daring way she'd ended her talk – Remember not one of the disciples believed in His Resurrection until the women dragged them there in the early morning and showed them the empty tomb, not one man believed until the women persuaded them of the truth, how often do you hear *that* mentioned? Not very! Probably those disciples were all asleep or getting ready to leave! Yes, it's always women who have had the strongest faith in Christ and His mystery. Oh, how Father Howard had frowned at that!

Afterwards they'd sat in the little cafe and talked, just the two of them, while the caretaker closed up around them. Once he asked them to leave, twice he asked them to leave, then he began to turn out the lights, it wasn't fair to delay the poor man so they stepped out onto the street and continued there, and why not, it was warm, it was dry, Colleen could always get the last train back to the hostel where she was staying. I don't want to give the impression it's all plain sailing Ali, there are ups and downs like anywhere else, almost everyone there went through a long discernment, years in some cases, but in the end it's so simple, you know my own decision was impossible, agonising, yet now it seems the easiest thing in the world – it might be the same for you, Ali, I have a feeling it will be. No reply this time from Alison. I can see it in you, Colleen continued, let's be honest the discernment is over, you've made up your mind, haven't you? Alison half nodded, the tears were coming and her eyes reddening. There's nothing to be afraid of, you can try it and leave any time, it's not like joining the army! Alison laughed, she wiped her eyes with the back of her hand, for a minute they stood in awkward silence, it was so hot still, the heat rising from the pavement, rising through her feet. Then, Have you heard anything of Edward? asked Colleen gently. Alison shook her head, from the immensity of the name she wished suddenly to curl up like a woodlouse under attack, this was the first time she'd heard it spoken aloud for

156

a long time, how pathetically thin her armour-plating was, how easily it cracked. You've been so brave, Colleen said, none of what happened was your fault. The two of them embraced, how young the girl was still, how beautiful, if only she'd take Alison away somewhere safe but it could happen, it could really happen, what was holding her back, only her own cowardice, take the next step Alison Forbes. All you have to do is knock on the door, Ali, dear Ali, whispered Colleen – Sister Colleen, RSCJ. Christ will guide you in everything else. They disentangled from each other, now would be a good moment to bid farewell, too much torment this, they're all talked out, time to get their regular faces back on. I've brought you a present, Colleen said, rummaging in her bag, but I don't know now, it might not be appropriate... Alison shrugged, anything from the girl would be appropriate, bound to be thoughtful, when it was offered she took it, a book, she'd look at it later. Don't tell Father Howard, he'd have something to say about it, the silly man, it's just a novel, very old, but it's about a couple, you see, one who believes and one who doesn't... we're not completely cut off where we are from things like novels. Thank you, I'll read it, I'm sure it'll be good. Well, I have to go for that train. Of course, you don't want to miss it. Well... goodbye. Goodbye Colleen – Sister Colleen. Goodbye, Sister Alison. – Oh don't! You'll have to run if you don't want to miss that train!

Now it was late at night, the temperature had eased, and Alison picked up the novel lying beside the Bible on her study desk. The house had been empty when she got back and apart from her it was empty still. Where was Joe? Already she'd prayed for him, active prayers, bring him home safe tonight, let him recover from the breakdown, let him recover fully. At least things had improved since the winter, how terrible those months had been, no accounting for the timing except to acknowledge that when sunlight was rare or non-existent it wasn't generally considered good for mental health. And then Joe had his hands full for so long keeping *her* afloat, something had had to give, in retrospect. But today was a blip, she needed to tell herself that, a setback, soon he'd be up and about, properly independent, plenty of summer sun to come and that would work wonders, plus it was true what she'd told him, the auras *were* becoming less frequent. It's not even that late, not if there's still light in the sky, he'll be back soon. She looked at the novel, The Heart of the Matter it was called. Odd choice of Colleen's, mostly it seemed to be about sin where it touched on religion at all but that wasn't her God and never once to her remembrance had she heard Colleen talk about sin. Their God was love, God in any case was unknowable and could only be approached through Christ Jesus, but then He too was love so what did it matter in the end. She read some lines here and there, it struck her as rather grim and negative and that was the last thing she needed. Oh well, there must be a reason Colleen gave it to me, I suppose I'll find out sooner or later. Into the single rickety drawer of the desk she slid the novel. She preferred the desktop to be empty of everything except the Bible and Cross.

What a poor place this box-room was, how limiting! Really nothing more than a desert. It shouldn't matter but somehow it did. And the truth, the barefaced shameless truth, she had to admit it, was that she'd outgrown Joe too. The new companion was her constant and preferred escort, He held her inside the cocoon of His love, He refused to leave, He was the witness of her changing and unchanging. Imagine saying it, imagine actually announcing it to Joe. It's only for a probation period, it only works out for very special people and I don't think I'm one of those, no it's not out of the blue, not really, I've been thinking about it for some time, you know I still correspond with Colleen, don't you? But imagining was one thing and doing it quite another. She took the Cross and pressed it to her heart. Perhaps the problem in recent times had been this never speaking of Edward's name, this pretending he'd never existed. It didn't work, it never had done, one simple mention out loud and everything got blown away, hearing it from Colleen's lips earlier was the proof. Harder she pressed the Cross, she dug it between her ribs, if the name Jesus contained all then the image must do too. None of it was your fault, Colleen had told her but Colleen didn't know everything. Again the tears were coming, again the memory, why did it keep coming back and torturing her, why had he kept doing it, dashing out into the road like that, again and again, driving me to distraction. Sometimes when you're a young mother you can hardly think straight. Five or six he must have been at the time, old enough to know better anyway, dear God what possessed me, the way I grabbed him and pushed him forward, I was in such a rage, all I wanted to do was frighten him when it came by so he wouldn't do it again but that bus driver should never have been driving so fast or close to the kerb. The way he went down sprawled out all arms and legs, a glancing blow I told myself afterwards, and yes he did get up straightaway but I never even took him to see the doctor, was that it, was that the cause of it?

Stop this. This appalling self-pity. She could not, would not, be pushed into those dark places again. It can't have been that, it can't – something peculiar to his mind instead. And even if it had been, hadn't he paid her back many times over? For in no way did a momentary loss of control caused by stress and with nothing ultimately behind it but dutiful protection equal in the great balance a premeditated plan of poisoning. No, guilt did not, could not, lie at the root of the encompassing love she felt for Christ and if even a single strand of that root had been stained with the blight then almost certainly it was some contamination of the Devil who once had worked directly through Edward but could do so now only via his memory. Through prayer then she would permit no growth of this single strand but rather encourage it to wither in order that it not jeopardise the grace which was changing her life and which she desired only to deepen. Yes, prayer was the way out, Sisterhood was the way out, she must listen to Colleen, if you wanted meaning in your life, peace, protection, anything like that, and if you sensed it in some particular place then to that place you must draw closer, you're obliged, you can't pull back, you can't pretend deafness. To be called and not to answer, what a terrible thing that would be.

But leaving Joe was another matter. Outgrowing did not mean abandoning. Not yet anyway. Who knows what had happened to make him walk out on Amanda Margaret like that and now stay out so late into the night. Whatever it was would have to be smoothed over. To think not so long ago she'd daydreamed about fixing the two of them up together. Let him rest some more then pull in the contacts, get in the work, liaise with customers, that was what a plumber's wife did. Make him see the doctor again. Everything done with the utmost kindness and generosity which was the very least he deserved. She laid the Cross flat on the desk, put both hands on the Bible and closed her eyes. Dear Lord, don't leave me behind, I'm making my way but the path is difficult. Grant me strength so that I may arrive sooner.

17

UNDER the flickering striplight that flattened everything so harshly the man Joseph moved aside his plumbing supplies. Those pieces which were metallic needed
careful handling in case they clashed with each other or
against the concrete floor of the garage, in these small
hours the slightest noise rang like the din of battle and
he didn't want to wake Alison who must be asleep inside
the house. If he'd been a carpenter instead he'd be hefting
soft lengths of wood about and not this crashing copper,
maybe there would be other upsides to it too, being
a carpenter, from his observations they never rushed
around like those in his trade, he suspected they got
more job satisfaction too. But then it was all about power
tools for them these days, the price of those things and
if you didn't buy the best you were only cutting off your
nose to spite your face. Of the copper bundles there
were many, they were taped together and stacked like
firewood, most plumbers would have exchanged them
for pounds at the municipal dump but not Joseph, there
was a purpose to their being arranged in this manner, for

behind them was concealed the box containing Edward's childhood photos and those few of his school books that Joseph had saved from Alison's purge. Here it was, he lifted it out, unclipped the plastic lid covered in dust and dead flies, there in wallets and folders was Edward, the baby-blob photos, mother and child just back from hospital, playground swings, at nursery, some of these captured moments Joseph remembered but most he didn't, stooping down he looked through every one. God if Alison should walk in now. Though in a way he hoped she would, he wanted to show her these, confront the failure to confront, remember how happy you were back then, you can't cancel this, you can't pretend it didn't happen. From his chest came a huhn-huhn-huhn judder, his lips fluttered, the snivel passed, what a state he must look, it had taken so long to find his way home, he felt on the point of collapse but now with his bed so near it was upon him powerfully, the shadow-bird of depression, breakdown, the mind-destructor, body-paralyser, those inside parts of himself which he needed in order to function in everyday life seemed to be drawing inexorably away, it was unbelievable how and to what dimensions the Edward-sized hole had grown since their midday encounter. More photos looked at, more unremembered things remembered, why is Joseph doing this to himself, why is he shopping for pain, if only at this late stage of our report we could find for him a moment of redemption, something missing made whole, but we can't, it isn't true.

When he put the box back and heaped the copper bundles over it the metal sounds of the re-heaping seemed to come from very far away. All he could think now was that giving the money to Edward had been a terrible mistake. £750, it was a lot, I'll pay you back, an invitation to return and no Mahdi's knife for him either, for surely that was gone for good. Capgras or no Capgras the kid was off his head, simple as that. So then he would be here to protect Alison, protection was the one thing he knew about, it was the one thing he could do. Softly he let himself into the house, softly he closed the door behind him and shot the bolt across. The light was on in the hall, the rest of the house dark and quiet, Alison's work drained her, to keep up with the demands of her promotion it was important she get her hours of sleep, how fortunate they were in having a slight surplus at the end of every month. Upstairs he tiptoed, he needed to wash, clean his cuts, quickly then, so tired, if she was in that deep dreamless state he wouldn't disturb her when he climbed into bed but so what if he did, a languorous night-time awakening might restore some of the intimacy they'd once had, why not embrace her, why not stroke her, what could be more natural for a couple who've been together as long as Joseph and Alison, their bodies held no secrets from each other. Alternatively they might talk, really talk, conversation in the dark, no moonlight, no streetlight, sometimes it's better not to see every nuance of the other person's face. I've found a way of living with all the things he did to me, she'd say, a way of going on, he's always there, he can't be forgotten but this is the arrangement I've come to, this is the settlement, I know it's been a mystery to you for a long time, now I'll share it, we can talk here in the dark for hours if you like, if it's necessary, I can see how agitated you are. Please tell me, he'd say, I want to hear it, your thoughts will help me, your reactions, be my friend, I think that's what I need most of all, today I saw him. Tell me everything. I will, I will. Or it might be that her slow-breathing body would have a calming effect on him, bring somnolence, even in sleep there's sometimes a gentle companionship. No, these things he dismissed, too much activity in his head despite the exhaustion of his body, more likely he'd wake her up with his fidgeting, something would be said that would be regretted, angry words at the wrong moment can wreak a lifetime's destruction. And then she looked so peaceful from the little of her he could see, from the outline he could see, her mouth slightly open, the rhythmic rustle of her throat was tranquillity itself.

He went along the landing to the box-room and went inside and turned on the light. Rarely did he enter this room, never was he invited. There crammed into the tiny space was the single bed he feared she'd begin to use one day, on the coverlet sat the furry lion and chewed fox from her childhood, her widebrimmed sunhat hung from a knobbed end of the curtain rail, no room here to pray, at least not pray as he imagined it, getting down on your knees. In its tight inconvenience it was like the restricted nook in which a plumber might work. Square in the centre of the miniature desk sat her Bible, on the dustjacketed cover a tree sprouted red leaves, no it was dropping them, surely the leaves should be green, the colour of rebirth, the colour of growth, wasn't that what religion was about, anyway they were red, this and the

Cross were the sources, the magical places from where she found the strength to deny Edward, the memory of him, the reality of him. All of a sudden he realised the idea had got fixed in his mind that she was ahead and he was faltering, always faltering, don't think like that, marriages aren't races, they don't work that way, yet he couldn't shake it off. Wretched Bible, you could make the words mean anything, terrible source of conflict in the world, better to burn this copy and all the rest. On a whim he opened the single drawer beneath the desktop. Another book – a novel. That was unusual, out of character. He picked it up, The Heart of the Matter it was called, and certainly that was a place he'd like to get to, certainly that was a location he'd like to reach. Typically it was about God, or a lot of it was about God, then as he flicked through the pages he saw a corner that had been turned down and turned up again, the lightest of creases, easy to miss, also a vertical pencil stroke next to some of the writing or there had been once, before being rubbed out. *Two of the new arrivals were the cannon fodder of all such occasions: elderly men with the appearance of plumbers who might have been brothers if they had not been called Forbes and Newall, uncomplaining men without authority, to whom things simply happened.*

18

FORGET Newall. That was just a name the author of this book had used to get his point across, to describe a man to whom things *simply happened*. A man of no importance. But the other name he'd chosen was Forbes. And Forbes was a plumber. And the passage had been marked, clearly marked, by Alison. It was incredible, also impossible it should be a coincidence. He had no idea why she'd erased the pencil mark, guilty conscience maybe, but that, in her secret heart, was what she thought of him. Edward had been allotted a single word, *demon.* Joseph's words were several: *man without authority. Uncomplaining. Elderly. Cannon fodder.*

For a long time he sat on the porridgey sofa downstairs. He sat with his eyes closed, with his eyes open. It isn't good, they say, for people to sit in the dark like this, it's human nature to always seek out the light, if we find a person acting this way we worry about them, it's a cause for concern. Possibly the clocks that were audible no longer played their happy roles of anti-annihilation, possibly they wished to hurry things on, not long now, not long now, not long till what, you'll see, you'll see. Into the sky outside came the first grey light of dawn and still Joseph was sat there, he hadn't nodded off, he hadn't gone to sleep. Around him the furniture of the front room or the lounge or the sitting room, whatever you have been brought up to call it, materialised, how cheap it was, how tawdry, it didn't seem fair to him that on the science programmes he watched occasionally on television professors should assert that the universe and its contents were nothing but swirling arrangements of atoms, or was it molecules, the tiny building blocks anyway, that nothing ever stayed still, that everything changed constantly, that wasn't his experience, one day after another you wake up and the food, the news, the parts of the body, the things you have to do, it's all the same as the day before and the day before that. Some journey to China, they acquire fortunes, people make statues of them, others pass through life like ghosts, barely visible from beginning to end, but nothing's a waste, we're told, nothing's a waste. What nonsense, what rubbish, everything's a waste, everything's futile, why not say it, why not admit it. Well then, in this dawn insubstantiality and cooling Joseph would become a ghost himself, let all hurtful things pass through him, a functional deadening only, he was halfway there already, in the tables of the human heart there aren't any rules about how alive you need to be inside or how vivid, monochrome is fine, sepia is fine, this was where the adventure of parenthood had left him.

GALLEY BEGGAR PRESS

We hope that you've enjoyed *Insignificance*. If you would like to find out more about James, along with some of his fellow authors, head to www.galleybeggar.co.uk.

There, you will also find information about our subscription scheme, 'Galley Buddies', which is there to ensure we can continue to put out ambitious and unusual books like *Insignificance*.

Subscribers to Galley Beggar Press:

· Receive limited black cover editions of our future titles (printed in a one-time run of 500)
· Have their names included in a special acknowledgement section at the back of our books.
· Are sent regular updates and invitations to our book launches, talks, and other events.
· Enjoy a 20% discount code for the purchase of any of our backlist (as well as for general use throughout our online shop).

WHY BE A GALLEY BUDDY?

At Galley Beggar Press we don't want to compromise on the excellence of the writing we put out, or the physical quality of our books. We've also enjoyed numerous successes and prize nominations since we set up in 2012. Almost all of our authors have gone on to be longlisted, shortlisted, or the winners of more than twenty of the world's most prestigious literary awards.

But publishing for the sake of art is a risky commercial strategy. In order to keep putting out the very best books we can, and to continue to support talented writers, we need your help. The money we receive from our Galley Buddy scheme is an essential part of keeping us going.

By becoming a Galley Buddy, you help us to launch and foster a new generation of writers.

To join today, head to
www.galleybeggar.co.uk/subscribe

FRIENDS OF GALLEY BEGGAR PRESS

Galley Beggar Press would like to thank the following individuals, without the generous support of whom our books would not be possible:

Ann Abineri
Kémy Ade
Timothy Ahern
Andrew Ainscough
Sam Ainsworth
Jez Aitchison
Callum Akaas
Ayodeji Alaka
Joseph H Alexander
Carol Allen
Richard Allen
Lulu Allison
Barbaros Altug
Kirk Annett
Eleanor Anstruther
Ebba Aquila
Elizabeth Aquino
Deborah Arata
Darryl Ardle
Robert Armiger
Sheila Armstrong
Sean Arnold
Curt Arnson
Xanthe Ashburner
Bethany Ashley
Robert Ashton
Adrian Astur Alvarez
Edmund Atrill
Vaida Aviks
Jo Ayoubi
Kerim Aytac
Claire Back
Andrew Bailey
Dexter Bailey
Tom Bailey
Edward Baines
Dawn Baird
Stephen Baird
Glynis Baker
Andrea Barlien
Chad Barnes
Ian Bartlett
Rachel Beale

James Beavis
Rachel Bedder
Joseph Bell
Angel Belsey
Felicity Bentham
Michelle Best
Gary Betts
David Bevan
Alison Bianchi
Benjamin Bird
Sandra Birnie
Peter Blackett
Matt Blackstock
Adam Blackwell
Melissa Blaschke
Lynne Blundell
David Boddy
Sophie Boden
John Bogg
Heleen Boons
Nicholas Bouskill
Poppy Boutell
Edwina Bowen
Michelle Bowles
Joanna Bowman
David Bradley
Sean Bradley
Andrew J. Bremner
Aisling Brennan
Joan Brennan
Amanda Bringans
Erin Britton
Julia Brocking
Ben Brooks
Dean Brooks
Lily Brown
Sheila Browse
Peter Brown
Carrie Brunt
Richard Bryant
Justine Budenz
Lesley Budge
Laura Bui

Tony Burke
Kevin Burrell
Alister Burton
Bryan Burton
Joyce Butler
Barbara Byar
Barry Byrne
Rebecca Café
Max Cairnduff
Alan Calder
June Caldwell
Lloyd Calegan
Christopher Caless
Alfric Campbell
Mark Campbell
Laura Canning
Joanna Cannon
Annette Capel
Rhian Capener
Thomas Carlisle
Leona Carpenter
Sean Carroll
Richard Carter
Shaun Carter
Stuart Carter
Soraya Cary
Liam Casey
Leigh Chambers
David Charles
Richard Chatterton
Marcus Cheetham
Rose Chernick
Lina Christopoulou
Neal Chuang
Neil Churchill
Enrico Cioni
Douglas
   Clarke-Williams
Steve Clough
Paul Cole
Faith Coles
Jennifer Coles
John Coles

Emma Coley
Sam Coley
Tonia Collett
Gordon Collins
Gerard Connors
Helene Conrady
Joe Cooney
Kenneth Cooper
Sarah Corbett
Paul Corry
Andy Corsham
Mary Costello
Sally Cott
Nick Coupe
Andrew Cowan
Diarmuid Cowan
Felicity Cowie
Isabelle Coy-Dibley
Matthew Craig
Nick Craske
Anne Craven
Emma Crawford
Anne-Marie Creamer
Alan Crilly
Joanna Crispin
Ian Critchley
Brenda Croskery
James Cross
Kate Crowcroft
Miles Crowley
Stephen Cuckney
Stephen Cummins
Andrew Cupples
HC
Emma Curtis Lake
Chris Cusack
Siddharth Dalal
Elisa Damiani
Rachel Darling
Rupert Dastur
Claudia Daventry
Mark Davidson
Harriet Davies
Jessica Davies
Linda Davies
Nickey Davies
Paul Davies
Alice Davis
Joshua Davis
Toby Day
Robin Deitch
Rebecca Demaree

Stanislaus Dempsey
Paul Dettmann
Turner Docherty
William Dobson
Dennis Donathan
Kirsty Doole
Kelly Doonan
Oliver Dorostkar
David Douce
Janet Dowling
Kelly Downey
Jamie Downs
Guy Dryburgh-Smith
Ian Dudley
Fiona Duffy
Florian Duijsens
Anthony Duncan
Antony Dunford
Stanka Easton
David Edwards
Nicola Edwards
Lance Ehrman
Jonathan Elkon
Ben Ellison
Ian Ellison
Thomas Ellmer
Stefan Erhardt
Alice Erskine
Fiona Erskine
Simeon Esper
Paul Ewen
Adam Fales
Monique Fare
Sarah Farley
Lori Feathers
Gerard Feehily
Jeremy Felt
Timothy Fenech
Michael Fenton
Charles Fernyhough
Edward J. Field
Paul Fielder
Joy Finlayson
Elizabeth Finn
Catriona Firth
Becky Fisher
Fitzcarraldo Editions
Holly Fitzgerald
Eleanor Fitzsimons
Alexander Fleming
Grace
    Fletcher-Hackwood

Hayley Flockhart
Nicholas Flower
Patrick Foley
James Fourniere
Ceriel Fousert
Richard Fradgley
Pauline France
Matthew Francis
Frank Francisconi
Emily Fraser
Annette Freeman
Emma French
Ruth Frendo
Melissa Fu
Graham Fulcher
Paul Fulcher
Lew Furber
Stephen Furlong
Michael Furness
Brid Gallagher
Timothy Gallimore
Marc Galvin
Annabel Gaskell
Honor Gavin
Michael Geisser
Phil Gibby
Alison Gibson
Nolan Geoghegan
Neil George
Andy Godber
James Goddard
Stephanie Golding
Elizabeth Goldman
Morgan Golf-French
Matthew Goodman
Sakura Gooneratne
Sara Gore
Nikheel Gorolay
Cathy Goudie
Simon Goudie
Emily Grabham
Paul Greaves
Louise Greenberg
Chris Gribble
Judith Griffith
Neil Griffiths
Ben Griffiths
Vicki Grimshaw
Sam Guglani
Robbie Guillory
Dave Gunning
David Gunning

Andrew Gummerson
Rhys Gwyther
Ian Hagues
Daniel Hahn
Alice Halliday
Peter Halliwell
Karen Hamilton
Emma Hammond
Paul Handley
Rachel Handley
Kirsteen Hardie
Hal Harding-Jones
Vanessa Harris
Jill Harrison
Alice Harvey
Becky Harvey
Shelley Hastings
Simon Hawkesworth
Sarah Hawthorn
Patricia Hayes
David Hebblethwaite
Richard Hemmings
Padraig J. Heneghan
Stu Hennigan
Penelope Hewett
    Brown
Felix Hewison-Carter
Martin Hickman
Alexander Highfield
Jennifer Hill
Molly Hill
Susan Hill
Daniel Hillman
Rod Hines
Alex Hitch
Marcus Hobson
Peter Hodgkinson
Camilla Hoel
Aisling Holling
Tim Hopkins
Shane Horgan
Rashad Hosein
William Hsieh
Hugh Hudson
Anna Jean Hughes
Emily Hughes
Gavin Hughes
Richard Hughes
Robert Hughes
Andy Hunt
Kim-ling Humphrey
Louise Hussey

LJ Hutchins
Simone Hutchinson
Simon Issatt
Joseph Jackson
Paul Jackson
Jane Jakeman
Hayley James
Gareth Jelley
Kavita A. Jindal
Alice Jolly
George Johnson
Jane Johnson
Bevan Jones
Emma Jones
Jupiter Jones
Kerry-Louise Jones
Rebecca Jones
Amy Jordison
Anna Jordison
Diana Jordison
Atul Joshi
Claire Jost
Benjamin Judge
Gary Kaill
Darren Kane
Laura Kaye
Thomas Kealy
Andrew Kelly
Michael Ketchum
Peter Kettle
Jeffrey Kichen
Vijay Khurana
Jacqueline Knott
Amy Koheealiee
Teddy Kristiansen
Elisabeth Kumar
Gage LaFleur
Philip Lane
Domonique
    Lane-Osherov
I Lang
Kathy Lanzarotti
Jackie Law
Jo Lawrence
Sue Lawson
Rick Le Coyte
Carley Lee
Liz and Pete Lee
Darren Lerigo
Joyce Lillie Robinson
Yin Lim
Rebecca Lake

Rachel Lalchan
Eric Langley
Catherine Latsis
Elizabeth Leach
Ferdia Lennon
Joanne Leonard
Chiara Levorato
Mark Lewis
Elizabeth Leyland
Christian Livermore
Jesse Loncraine
Katie Long
Nick Lord Lancaster
Isaac Lowe
Lele Lucas
Sean Lusk
Simona Lyons
Marc Lyth
Jean Mackay
Wendy and Dave
    MacKay
Victoria MacKenzie
Andrea Macleod
Duncan Mackie
Brendan Madden
Joseph Maffey
Anne Maguire
Eleanor Maier
Johnny Mains
Philip Makatrewicz
Anil Malhotra
Tom Mandall
Joshua Mandel
Matthew Mansell
Emily Marchant
Chiara Margiotta
Natalie Marshall
Paul Marshall
Iain Martin
Amanda Mason
Rosalind May
Philip Maynard
Stephen Maynard
Sally Mayor
Sara McCallum
Amy McCauley
Paul McCombs
Ella McCrystle
Fabia McDougall
Kieran McGrath
Sheila McIntosh
Alan McIntyre